THE ITINERARY

PENNY PENTLEY

Cover artwork includes images from MM Memo, TheAnts, Sidney Hendriks, Awwa Studio, and Radoz Design on Canva.

ISBN: 979-8-9876498-2-4 (paperback)

Published by Five Cents Publishing

Dedication

Mom,
Thank you for sharing your love of travel.
"Penny" (a.k.a. the Stockholm Airport – ARN)

Chapter 1

My day—night?—starts as I'm jolted awake from my half-sleep by wheels on the tarmac. I didn't really rest much with all the turbulence, but I dozed off enough to pass the time, I suppose. My mom had been adamant that we book a nonstop "so we can sleep," but that definitely didn't happen—the "sleep" part or the "we" part.

My mom wanted to take this trip in honor of Dad, but I guess they should tell you the statistics of a widow dying within a year of their spouse when you book your "spending Dad's retirement fund" trip.

But Mom made me promise to go "no matter what." She even booked non-refundable tickets. I tried to persuade my sister Alice to go with me, but she lives across the country with a job and infant twins. It was hard enough for her to make it home for two funerals in a twelve-month span.

So here I am, alone, sitting by a stranger who took my mom's seat on standby. Either he wears the same cologne as my mom's old boss or that smell is coming from me. I guess I never got around to washing this sweater after all the hugs at the funeral. I mean, it was only a week ago, and I didn't expect to bring what I wore to bury both of my parents, but when I walked by the chair it was lying on, I could hear my mom's voice hollering, "Bring a sweater!" Not literally, because that would have been freaking creepy, but you know what I mean. Anyway, it came in handy when the flight attendants ran out of blankets and I realized my stretch jeans and baggy shirt weren't going to cut it.

I am brought back to the present by the ding of the seatbelt sign turning off. Of course, everyone around me immediately stands up, but I know it will take forever for everyone to file out, so I get to work organizing my bag—making sure my passport is right at the top for easy access. I need organization. In my space, in my life. I know where everything is and what's going to happen.

Despite never having traveled intercontinentally before and knowing absolutely no Italian, I manage to navigate the airport pretty well. My uneasiness about doing this alone is squashed by my confidence in my ability to logically tackle any situation, even on a limited amount of sleep.

However, what greets me at baggage claim gives me an awful omen about this trip. Well, what *doesn't* greet me, that is. I don't even realize it until the belt has been stopped for a good five minutes and everyone else from my flight is long gone.

"Orlando?" I yell, quickly catching myself and dropping down to a whisper. "What is my bag doing in Orlando?"

"I am not sure," the gate agent says in perfect English, but with a heavy Italian accent. "Rome is FCO and Orlando MCO. Perhaps that has something to do with this?"

"But there's barcodes and computers doing this stuff. How did it get sent to the wrong airport in the 21st century?" I take a deep breath. I don't want to be a Karen. "Do you know how long it will take to get my bag here?"

The man behind the desk taps at his computer, pursing his lips. He clicks his tongue a few times before saying, "If you would have gotten here ten minutes sooner, we could have had it tomorrow, but now it looks like the best we can do is Monday."

"Monday?" I shriek. Really, I can't help it, seeing as how it's currently *Friday*.

"Yes, Signora West. Our baggage delivery team does not work on Sundays. If you wish to return to the airport, it can be waiting for you on Sunday, but we cannot deliver it until Monday."

Trek all the way back to the airport to get my bags one day earlier? Might not be worth it. Besides, they offered some money to get myself new clothes—it may be fun to do some shopping in Italy. A realization hits me. "I'll be in Florence on Monday."

"Then we can deliver your bag there. Just give us the address of your hotel." He slides over a piece of paper and I finish the first hour of my two-week European getaway filling out paperwork.

Customs is fun. Apparently a single person arriving in a foreign country with no luggage is crazy suspicious. I have to explain to, like, three different people that my bag just didn't show up. One of them even calls the airline to confirm, despite my having paperwork explaining everything.

At least there's no line for the taxi stand. It may technically be early afternoon, but I just want to get to my hotel and sleep.

With traffic, it takes about an hour to get into the city. I want to be excited about all the ruins and sights we drive by, but honestly, my blood sugar and energy levels are too low to care.

A few turns down ungodly-narrow alleys and the taxi driver drops me off at my hotel. He opens the trunk, then shuts it again. Just habit to go get the luggage, I guess.

Unassuming from the outside, the hotel is gorgeous once I enter. The dark wood furniture is accented with shining bronze. It screams "cozy" in a terribly elegant way.

"Lisa West," I say, placing my ID on the front desk.

The receptionist stares at me wide-eyed. "Buongiorno."

A few beats later, we are still staring at each other. "Buongiorno," I finally think to repeat.

"You are...checking in?" she asks in labored English.

I let out a relieved sigh. I half thought she was going to tell me my reservation didn't exist. "Yes. My name is Lisa West and I am checking in."

She consults her screen. "Lisa West e Diane West?"

My heart stops at hearing my mom's name. "No, only Lisa West."

The receptionist gathers some paper and a key from a cabinet behind her. "Your wife is coming more late?" She hands me the packet.

"No, my *mother*..." I fade off, not wanting to explain, but the receptionist must see the tears in my eyes.

"Sono desolata, signora." She puts her hand on mine, waiting there a moment before shifting to a less solemn demeanor. "Your room...up two stairs, two one two."

"Two twelve. Thank you. Uhh...grazie."

I look up the narrow staircase, sort of relieved I don't have to lug my baggage up there. That relief only lasts half of a second before I remember I only have one pair of clean underwear in my carry-on. I rub my temples. That's a tomorrow problem. Right now, I am hiking up these stairs. The second flight isn't as long as the first, thank goodness, but my calves are still screaming when I finally get to my room. I unlock the door to a simple room with two twin beds neatly made. I open the small window, lay down in the bed closest to the fresh air, and pass out to the sounds of the busy Italian alley below.

Chapter 2

I wake up to the glow of sunlight creeping between buildings, accented by the beeps of trucks backing up. Morning. Did I really beat jet lag on day one? I doubt it; it will surely come back to bite me later. I toss a bit in the bed, realizing it actually *is* comfortable, it wasn't just my exhaustion.

When I finally peel myself out of bed, I clean myself up in the tiny shower and put on my only change of clothes—some jean shorts and a baggy tank top. They'll look interesting with the ankle boots I wore on the plane. Thank goodness my mom sent me that article about what to pack in your carry-on, though, otherwise I wouldn't have thought to bring a change of clothes at all.

My hair still wet, I make my way down to the lobby for breakfast. I down four glasses of water—I guess I never rehydrated properly after that flight. I eat some hard-boiled eggs and bread with jam. In front of me lies the first page of the itinerary my mom had hand-written for this trip on tiny notebook paper. I didn't have the heart to look it over until now.

Rome, Day 1:
Arrive FCO 1:00 pm
Private car FCO to Hotel, prepaid

My jaw drops. *Did I really just leave a driver waiting for me at the airport?* No, he would have called my mom to confirm, right? When he didn't get a hold of her he must have canceled the booking… The "itinerary" is seriously lacking any detail, but my mom did email me all the train and hotel confirmations, so I guess this will have to do. I continue reading:

Rome, Day 2:
Drink real Italian espresso
Look at old stuff (Colosseum? Forum?)
Eat pasta
Find a cute European guy for Lisa

I nearly spit out my water when I read the last one. But really, who writes plans like this? When am I going where? My mom loved to go with the flow, but she did know who she was taking this trip with, right? All of that aside, I know I at least want to go see some old stuff and probably have pasta, but I also need to do a shopping trip first.

I open the guidebook my mom used to plan this part of the trip—*Bob Adams' Adventures: Europe*. It is worn and tabbed and highlighted to heck, but I plan on using my mom's notes as my compass, guiding me on the trip she wanted to take. I start to cry when I see a little scrawl next to a site: "Lisa would love this."

The family at the table next to mine gives me strange looks, so I finish up my last few bites and start up the stairs. I manage to save the big part of the breakdown for after I close the door to my room.

I wash my face in cold water to ease the puffiness under my eyes. I had to skip my big cry yesterday since I was 30,000 feet over the Atlantic, so it came on twice as strong this time. Maybe it wouldn't hurt so much if it wasn't so sudden. With Dad, we knew for weeks that he was going to die. Mom? She was only able to hold on long enough for Alice to say goodbye over the phone. I shake my head. *Happy trip. Happy trip.*

I head down to reception with my guidebook in my day bag—a small backpack I sling over one shoulder. There is a young man working now. "Buongiorno, would you be able to help me find somewhere to buy some clothes? My luggage got lost."

The receptionist's face falls.

Oh no. Not again. "I'm sorry. Do you speak English?"

"I do, Signora. I am sorry to tell you that most stores are closed today for the Feast of Ferragosto."

My brain takes a second to catch up while I stand there in silence. "So I have to wait another day to have clean clothes?"

He presses his lips together, giving a pained squint. "Many stores are closed on Sunday, as well; especially after a holiday."

"Are you saying that I have to wear these clothes for three days?" I could already feel my skin getting sticky in the August humidity and, while the tank top I'm in is pretty light and flowy, I don't think it will stay fresh for *three days.*

"You might find some shirts in tourist shops. They are usually open. And the pharmacy may have some more delicate items." A flush comes across his cheeks at the last line.

"Can you get me directions to the nearest pharmacy, then?" I pull out my guidebook, open to a tabbed page, and point at the words *Campo de Fiori*. "And directions here, too, please."

He pulls out a paper map, showing me where we are, where the Campo—which is basically a town square—is, and the location of a pharmacy along the way. "It is a bigger shop, so they may have more of what you need."

I stare hard at the streets I want to take, knowing that taking a map out at a tourist site is just an invitation for pickpockets. Once I think I know the way, I fold up the map and tuck it into my bag with my guidebook. "Grazie."

"Prego. Welcome to Italy!"

His call follows me to the door, where I step out into the alleyway. It hits me: I'm in Rome! A huge, dopey smile spreads across my face as I start my walk.

I wind through a handful of side streets before turning a corner to see an enormous church on a major boulevard. I take a left, as instructed, and see the flashing neon green cross that indicates my first destination. I pop inside and get an immediate chill—the AC is probably on full blast in anticipation of the heat coming this afternoon.

Getting my bearings, I try to spot where I'm headed, but my heart falls when I realize this is no CVS or RiteAid. No flip flops to save my poor feet or undershirts I can pass off as actual shirts. My saving grace is a "travel size" display with sample packs of pain relievers, shampoo, toothpastes, and...laundry soap. *Sink laundry it is, then.* I snag a tiny detergent, some Tums, and a travel dental care kit before heading up to the register. It was only after seeing the display that I realized just how gross my mouth is.

Continuing on my planned route, one of the alleys that takes me to the square is lined with tourist shops. That's a good sign that I'm getting close, right? The shirts hanging from the awnings of these tiny businesses are...tacky...to say the least, from huge print "Roma" or "Italia" across the front to "Ciao Bella" written in the same font as a popular soda brand. There's also a bunch of soccer jerseys, most likely knockoffs, emblazoned with the names of people I've never even heard of, seeing as how I don't really like soccer.

I'll save that as a last resort.

As I step into the plaza, I am greeted by swarms of tour groups. Flags and light sticks poke into the air as a gaggle of white-haired retirees in visors follow them around. If old folks can take a tour from here, it must be pretty walkable to other sites, right? I find a seat at a cafe and pull out my tour book. Sure enough, there is a whole four pages titled "Walking Tour from Campo de Fiori."

A beautiful, young waitress with sleek, black hair approaches, asking me in English what I'd like. It's no surprise that I stick out as a tourist, sitting with a guidebook at a cafe in a popular tourist spot. I ask for a latte. I know my mom wanted me to shoot straight espresso, but I'm not sure my stomach can take it after the stress of yesterday. While I wait, I study the walking route and catch my bearings. The route should take me past the Pantheon and end on the Spanish Steps—both things my mom highlighted in the book. When the drink arrives, I close my book and simply watch the world around me. I drink in the caffeine and the atmosphere simultaneously. There must have been some kind of farmer's market this morning since some trucks are packing up the last of the tables and awnings. Hopefully I didn't miss anyone selling undergarments alongside their tomatoes.

A sweet old couple at the next table waves to get my attention, breaking me from my musings.

"Pardon, miss," the woman says, her southern drawl coating every word. "My husband and I were going to shop the market today, but it turns out it closed early for the holiday. If it wouldn't be too much of a bother, could we borrow your *Bob Adams* to see what else we can do instead?" She points at the book sitting by my coffee.

"No, not at all!" I run my fingers over the tabs. "My mom marked a bunch of stuff she was interested in. Maybe the marked pages will give you a good start." I pause for a moment before handing it to her.

"Well, bless you and your mother." Her smile turns saccharine as she has to tug a little extra hard to pull the book from my grasp.

I try to continue my zoning-out session from before, but my eyes keep flashing back to the couple. The wife is oooh-ing and aah-ing a bunch of different sites, while the husband gives out noncommittal grunts, though something in his eyes tells me he enjoys seeing his wife so excited.

When they're done, they hand the book back, a huge grin on the wife's face. "I think today is the day we see the Trevi

Fountain!" She leans in close to me and whispers, "Rumor is that if you toss in two coins, you'll fall in love. I already have my hubby, so these are for you." She sets two Euro coins on my table and waves. After they've gone, I stare at the two coins. *I guess I'll have to visit the Trevi Fountain at some point.* I put them into a special pocket of my purse.

After an awkward exchange with the waitress—apparently tipping isn't a thing here—I head off to my route. Actually, I head in the exact opposite direction of where I'm supposed to go. As I return back across the square, I pray nobody recognizes me as the woman who had just so purposefully walked the other way.

The walk takes me through a few more town squares, each with its own unique charm, but I am in awe when I reach Piazza Navona. It gives the vibe of a university quad, but older and more important. If the incredibly loud tour guide I walk by is to be believed, it used to be a racetrack way back in the day.

When people move to Rome, I wonder how long it takes them to get used to the scale of everything. The craftsmanship, the age, the cultural significance of everything around them. Do kids take it for granted that they drink from a fountain once fed by ancient aqueducts? Do they scoff and say, "Eh, it's only five hundred years old," because the building down the street was built at the turn from BC to AD? Meanwhile, our oldest buildings are crumbled log frames from two hundred years ago, if that.

It's not much farther to the Pantheon. I join the line of people, bending around the fountain out front, waiting to enter, and am quickly sandwiched in between two families. The ones in front seem...done. Two of the teenagers in their group are arguing with their parents about something. I have no idea what any of them are saying, or even what language they're speaking, but it is clearly a passionate debate, given the volume and excessive hand gestures. The other teenager is glued to his phone, either oblivious to the shouting match or intentionally ignoring it. A pang of grief strikes through my gut. Every fiber of me wants to tell these kids to appreciate this time with their family.

I peek around them and find the line isn't moving at all. I don't want to be an audience to this argument anymore, so I decide to come back to the Pantheon later and finish the walking tour then. Looking at the map, I am pretty close to the hotel, anyway. It might be a good time to grab lunch and catch a nap, given this wave of tiredness that has suddenly overwhelmed me. I know I should have a strict schedule and stick to it, but that cozy bed just sounds so nice.

On the walk back, I snag a sandwich and a soda from a shop. The sun beating directly down onto the streets is draining every last remaining bit of energy I have, so a sit-down meal might not be the best idea unless I want to fall asleep on a bed of spaghetti.

I sit alone on the foot of my bed, trying not to spill crumbs on my sheets, watching the only English-speaking channel I can find on my tiny in-room television—BBC. Next thing I know, it is an hour later, I am drooling onto the sheets, and the half of the sandwich I never got around to eating is face-down on the carpet. *So much for beating jet lag.*

Gravity fights me as I try to get off of the bed and into the bathroom to wash yesterday's clothes. Well, tomorrow's clothes. I let them soak for a few minutes in soapy water, then scrub the important bits, before rinsing and hanging them on the shower curtain rod. It will just have to do.

I take the shortcut back to the Pantheon, spending almost two hours in there, watching the spotlight of the sun through the roof slowly creep across the inside of the building. Honestly, my mom would have hated it. She couldn't sit still to save her life, always on the go, trying anything and everything. I am much more content to just watch and contemplate, if there is enough time to do so.

I buy a cold bottle of water to take with me on the rest of the route. It is a long way, and even though the tall buildings block some of the sunlight, they also block any breeze, making this sweat accumulating in my clothes almost useless.

A few more piazzas later, I finally make it to the Trevi Fountain. It is gorgeous, of course—a magnificent feat of sculpture and water. I play with the two coins the woman gave me this morning as I bob and weave through the crowd making their wishes and throwing their coins. Seeing an opening to the right, I swing around to the side of the fountain and get a spot right at the front. I close my eyes, turn around, and throw the coins over my shoulder, one at a time, wishing for a trip my mom would have loved. Just as I open my eyes, a coin smacks me on my right cheek. It sticks on there for a second, thanks to the glistening sweat coating my entire body, then falls to the ground. Not wanting someone to lose out on a wish of their own, I toss it over my shoulder, too, and I can hear it *plop* into the water behind me.

As much as I want to stand and watch people make their wishes that, honestly, probably won't come true, I quickly become very aware of the smell of this crowd. It seems everyone has been walking a lot in this heat, but not everyone has found time to reapply deodorant. I push back out of the throng, ending up by a cute little fountain that people are drinking out of. My water bottle is empty, so I decide to refill it, having read that the public fountains in Rome are safe to drink from and, hey, *when in Rome.* There are two streams of water that cross in the middle, so I hold my water bottle right in the center, seeing if I can refill it twice as quickly to get out of the way for the line of couples that forms behind me.

The sun is just starting to dip as I make my way north to the Spanish Steps. I am hit with the tantalizing smell of carbs and butter. I'd already looked up the place I wanted to eat dinner, complete with reviews and a look over the menu to tentatively decide what I wanted, but something in the back of my mind was screaming that *this right here* is what I need. I look down at a plate a waiter has just set down. Noodles with cheese and pepper. Really? That's it? My stomach responds with a gurgle almost loud enough to be heard by passers-by on this busy street.

I ask for a table.

"Per due?" the waiter asks, holding up two fingers.

I shake my head and hold up one. "Just me."

He shrugs and leads me to a table further from the edge of the outdoor seating area. I suppose sad tourists eating alone is not a huge draw for people walking by. Regardless, I manage to find the meal on the menu and order myself some sparkling water. Did I want sparkling water? No. Do I like sparkling water? No. Is that what I'm drinking with my meal? Yes, because I asked for a bottle of water, and technically he brought me a bottle of water, so no use arguing. Lesson learned. I still have half my refilled bottle from before, anyway. Next time I'll just order a Coke or something.

As I take my first bite of the meal, my brain nearly short-circuits with how this seemingly simple dish fills every culinary desire I have at this moment. Carby, fatty, salty—as I get to my last bite I begin to contemplate how appropriate it is to lick the bowl clean. I begrudgingly decide against it, instead paying my bill—no tip this time—and leaving to find something sweet to cap the night off before heading back to the hotel.

Gelato in hand, I decide to eat on the Spanish Steps, joining the gaggle of couples and young folk who are relaxing and finishing their night. The sky is slowly shifting to darker and darker shades. A rideshare back is likely the best option, so I open my phone and make sure I still have the app downloaded—I hardly ever go out at home, so there's never much of a need.

I take my last bite of stracciatella and lean back on the stairs, looking up at the emerging stars in the clear sky. "I wish you were here, Mom," I whisper, but this is not my mom's trip. My mom would go crazy just sitting and watching the world go by. Sure, she'd love to spend twenty minutes commenting on the couples, making theories as to how they met or what they're doing in Rome, but she would want to do something big, something completely spur-of-the-moment. I smile, promising to do one impulsive thing in Rome.

"Pub crawl!" A voice shouts in an American accent from the bottom of the stairs. "Pub crawl starts at nine from the bar with the green awning!"

Chapter 3

"Twenty euros to join and your first drink is free," the host says as I approach him at the bar.

I could still back out, but this doesn't seem too bad. It's casual, so if I need to bail at any point, I can. Plus, it looks like a bunch of college kids with some folks in their 30s and 40s thrown in for flavor—at least I won't be the oldest person there. I hand him a twenty.

"Just you?" He asks, not looking up from the buttons he is pressing on a tablet.

"Uh..." I pause, not about to let someone know I'm going to be intoxicated while traveling alone. "No, my friends..." I give a noncommittal response while vaguely gesturing to the small group waiting at the bar.

He gives a sideways nod, signaling for me to make my way inside. I wait at the bar to get my first drink of the night—my first drink of the trip, actually. How have I not had any alcohol yet? The group of college kids seem like they got a head start on the festivities.

"Like this chick." One of the twenty-somethings with bleach-blonde hair grabs my arm and pulls me into their circle.

Her drunkenness slurs her words even more than her unidentifiable accent does. "She gets it, right?"

All eyes are on me. I turn to the woman and ask, "I get what?"

Her face lights up. "And she's Canadian!"

The whole group hoots at that news.

"American, actually," I correct, wondering how the vibe will change with that revelation.

"American!" The girl nearly screams, throwing her drink into the air, spilling something fruity on my arm, as the rest of the group joins in the cheer. When the excitement dies down, she adds, "Then you *definitely* get it."

One of her male friends meets my gaze, sympathy in his chestnut eyes, then inserts himself between me and the woman. "Sorry about Mads. I think she is still drunk from our outing last night." His accent is clearly French, and definitely not as slurred as his friend's.

"Am not!" Mads nudges him with her elbow, spilling even more of her drink.

"I am Luc and *this*—" he reaches over to the bar and takes a shot glass from a tray, "—is for you. To apologize for having to smell like whatever sugary mess this is."

I inspect my arm, smelling it. I can't even identify what drink it might be, but I can feel the sugar sticking to my skin. Luc is still holding the shot glass out, but I hesitate. Open beverage from a complete stranger? Red flag. But I did see the bartender pour the shots as I was approaching the bar. Then again, I was distracted for a little while in between then and now. He could have easily slipped something into it. I take the glass, peeking into the liquid. Nothing floating or dissolving, just clear alcohol.

Luc's eyebrows raise and he takes the glass back, shooting it himself. He makes eye contact with the bartender, pointing at the empty shot. "Can we have one more of these?"

Within seconds, I have a fresh shot in my hand. I shoot it back, my face contorting as I realize this is tequila, not vodka, like I assumed. I cough a few times once it's down.

Luc pats me on the back, laughing. "You are welcome to join us, you and your friends..." He scans the bar for my traveling companions.

Don't tell people you're traveling alone. "Oh, they're meeting me further down the crawl. I'd love to group up until they get here." I get myself my drink and get to know the team.

Mads is from South Africa, Luc from France, then Thomas and Louis are cousins from Switzerland, Jamie and Jenny are twins from the States, and Mateo is from Spain. They get along like old friends, but it turns out they are simply staying at the same hostel and only met this week.

Don't quiz me later on the names and lands of origin, because there is no way I'll remember tomorrow. You'd expect them to make the drinks really weak, trying to keep our endurance up, but at the first three bars we went to, they were very heavy-handed pours. I feel like I'm back in college myself, and while I'm nowhere near where Mads is, I am getting quite drunk. Part of me feels like this might be a good time to tap out, but I also have this wave of energy that I don't normally have at eleven at night. Plus, I'm not sure I want to leave this group so soon. Luc has been so welcoming and, while he was cute when I met him, he just keeps looking better and better at each bar. He also gets more and more cozy with me as the time goes by. From a hand on the small of my back to help guide me through a crowd, to his arm rubbing against mine as we stand chatting, to his arm around my shoulder as we walk between stops—all of it very welcome. It's been a while since a guy has shown me this kind of attention.

As we enter the fourth bar, Mads holds her hand over her mouth, wide-eyed, and books it for the restroom at the back of the bar. Luc laughs, looking at his watch. "Eleven fifteen! Mateo, you're buying this round."

Mateo pulls out a hundred Euro note and hands it to Luc. "That girl is not from South Africa."

Jenny steps up to the bar first, ordering an "acqua naturale" before turning back to the group. "That girl has been drinking for 24 hours. It doesn't matter where you're from, the human stomach can only handle so much."

Luc asks for my order. I probably should slow down, since my lips and cheeks are already a bit numb, but I'm having fun, so I decide to try to keep the buzz going.

He hands me my rum and coke, then takes my hand and leads me to a booth. It's the first time we are alone all night and his body is pressed up against mine, despite the booth having more than enough space for four people. I can smell the sugar and rum on his breath as he leans in close and whispers, "I am so glad your friends are not here yet."

I bite my lip and drop my voice, too. "I'm actually here alone."

He pushes himself even closer to me and I can feel his body heat through his clothes. "Then you should come back to the hostel with us. This city is safer in a group."

His face is so close to mine, and I do something impulsive. I'm pretty sure I spill some of my drink down the back of his neck as I pull his face toward mine, but it doesn't faze him. He simply reaches behind his head and takes my drink, setting it on the table as he pushes forward, pinning me to the seat.

I am overwhelmed with two sensations: the fake leather sticking to the back of my legs and Luc's tongue working its way past my numb lips. I focus on the kissing, but my mind keeps getting distracted. We're pretty in the open here. In fact, I can hear whooping from someone at the bar. I start to laugh, but Luc continues, escalating the kiss into a full-blown make-out session. My body responds, getting riled up in all the right places, and wanting to do *all of the things* with this guy I just met today.

When his hand slides up my inner thigh, I have a sudden burst of clarity and push him away. "What are you doing?"

"Kissing you." He leans in again, kissing my neck. "Touching you." His hand moves toward my chest and I push it away.

"In public?" A nervous laugh escapes with the question.

He smiles, shrugging. "I suggested going to the hostel, but you seemed ready to do something here."

I scoot a little further away from him, feeling a little claustrophobic backed up in the booth. "I just met you. I'm not going to do something with someone I just met."

Luc's smile falls. Without a word, he leaves the booth and goes back to the group. "Let's go back to the hostel. This place is dead."

I can just barely hear Jenny ask, "What about Lisa?"

Luc pushes everyone toward the door, facing them away from me. "She is not coming."

Most of the group goes along with it, but Jenny turns and gives me a sad wave before leaving.

I give a weak wave back to accompany my half-hearted smile. The volume in the bar cuts in half when they all depart and a ringing in my ears becomes the primary sound. Luc's drink and mine are on the table in front of me and I pound both. Turns out that his was a double.

I sulk in the booth for a few more minutes, watching everyone else enjoying their Saturday night. The alcohol kicks in even harder and, though I don't think I'm going to end up worshiping the porcelain goddess like Mads, I should definitely order my rideshare before I lose what's left of my composure. I pull out my phone, but the apps on my screen seem to blur together. Probably from the brightness. It's pretty dark in here. I stare for a few seconds until I give up and click my screen off. I'll wait it out.

A man sits down across from me in the booth. "Are you going to be okay getting back to your hotel?" His voice is flavored with a standard American accent and a dash of pity.

I blink a few times and his features become clear. Short, dirty blonde hair, and a charming smile. I know this guy. I *swear* I've seen this guy before. "Do I know you?"

"No. Sorry." He points over his shoulder to a table in the middle of the bar. "I was just sitting there and saw what happened. I want to make sure you're able to get to where you need to go."

I wince. "How much did you see?"

"You're not exactly in a secluded corner over here. Now, can I help you get a taxi or something?"

I grab my purse and shuffle through it, trying to find my phone. "No, I think I can get a ride on my phone. I just need...to find it..." Did I seriously just lose my phone in the past two minutes?

The stranger picks my phone up off the table and reaches over for my hand. His skin is warm and soft on mine as he guides my finger to the fingerprint scanner. "I'll help. Where are you going?"

"My hotel," I shoot back with a bite of stubbornness.

"Good call. I wouldn't recommend going to another bar. What hotel, though?"

I freeze. What is the name of my hotel? "I..." My eyes scan the table as if the answer is ingrained in the wood.

"Oh, Lord." He takes my purse and pulls out my plastic water bottle still half-filled with the fountain water. He opens it and hands it to me. "Drink."

I eye it skeptically. "How do I know you didn't do something to it?"

He stares at me, his green eyes deadpan as he takes a large sip himself, then hands it back to me.

I take it, nursing baby sips so I don't overwhelm my poor stomach.

The stranger reaches back into my bag, pulling out my *Bob Adams' Adventures*. He lets out a short, loud laugh.

"It's my mom's." I pull the purse back away from him.

He opens to one of the tabbed pages. "Sure…" After thumbing through it a bit, he holds an open page to me, pointing at one of the hotels with stars drawn in next to it. "Is this it?"

It sounds familiar. Really familiar. About as familiar as this guy looked. "Yeah. That's it. But really, don't I know you from somewhere?"

He types the address into my phone, presses a few more buttons, and slides it back across the table to me. "Leo will be here in five minutes."

I squint at him, trying to figure it out. "What's your name?"

"Rocky."

"Rocky? Like…" I throw two punches, one of them catching on the rim one of the empty glasses. The glass is fine, but I have to grab the side of my hand to stop the sudden burst of pain.

"Yeah, or like the alien in…" he trails off. "Never mind. That would be a spoiler if you ever wanted to read that book."

"What book?"

His eyes go wide. "Spoiler. I'm not telling you."

"No, but you look *so* familiar."

"What can I say? Generic white guy face." He hands me back my travel book and stands, holding out his hand to help me up.

I use the table for support instead, waving him off when I make it upright. "Thanks for your help, but I think I got it from here."

Rocky takes a step back. "Absolutely. Have a good night."

I make it out front just as my ride arrives. The cobblestones were rough enough to navigate before in these heeled ankle boots, but even harder now that I am officially drunk. I look like a mess as I stumble into the car and give the driver my code. It's not much longer until I am back at the hotel. Two precarious flights of stairs later, I'm in my bed, passing out almost the second my head hits the pillow.

Chapter 4

The concentrated sunlight hitting my face is not a welcome visitor. My veins feel like they have battery acid flowing through them. My head is swimming. Lying in bed, I contemplate going back to sleep, but it's my last day in Rome and I want to make it count. The Colosseum? The Forum? My mom wanted to see old stuff, but I cringe at the idea of being out in the heat right now.

I sit up. Step one is dealing with this hangover, *then* I can decide what to do with my day. I throw on my jean shorts that still smell of alcohol and the hand-washed black top and underwear I wore on the airplane and go downstairs for breakfast, which ends in fifteen minutes. The ankle boots I've been wearing for the past two days are starting to feel uncomfortable and blisters are forming. That's what I get for wearing my bulkiest shoes on the plane so more could fit into my suitcase. I focus on breakfast instead: plain toast for now, maybe a little bit of juice. Don't want to risk it. I freeze at the bottom of the stairs when I see a familiar face.

Rocky stands up from the leather chair he was waiting in, leaving a large yellow notepad on the seat. "Hi."

I take a few tentative steps toward him. "Hi?"

"Sorry if this is weird. I just wanted to make sure you got back alright. I asked at the front desk, but they couldn't help since I didn't know your name." He shrugs. "So I waited."

I give myself a once-over. "I seem to be in one piece."

"Good. Good." He looks back at his seat.

"How long have you been waiting here?"

He looks at his watch. "Just about two hours. I didn't think you'd be up before eight."

I scratch the back of my head, my fingers getting tangled in the unbrushed mess of hair. "Yeah, I did a lot of...walking...yesterday."

He narrows his eyes. "Walking. Yeah. That'll do it."

"Yeah. Thanks again for your help last night—" I point to the dining room, "—but I have to get to breakfast before ten."

"Don't let me stop you. I was just making sure you were good." He goes to his chair and starts to fiddle with a computer bag and his notepad.

Just as I'm turning around, an impulse draws me back. "Lisa."

He looks up from packing his bag. "Lisa?"

"In case you need to check up on me again."

"Short for Elizabeth?"

"Yes, but with an 's.'"

"Elissssabeth?" He hisses his s.

"No," I stop him, no humor in my tone. "Just Elisabeth."

He gives a polite nod and zips his bag. "Until next time, Lisa."

I want to say something in return, but repeating "until next time" feels strange, since I will probably never see this man again in my entire life. I just wave instead and rush to the dining

room where the staff are already tidying up the buffet. I grab
a few pieces of bread as they're pulling the basket away, as well
as a hard-boiled egg. My stomach handles it as well as can be
expected, so I grab an orange juice and head back upstairs to
wash tomorrow's clothes in the sink.

Once everything is clean-*ish*, I rummage through my purse.
As I pull out my *Bob Adams*, my mom's itinerary falls out with
it. I look back on Day Two's plan.

> Day 2:
> Drink real Italian espresso? *Check.*
> Look at old stuff? *Check.*
> Eat pasta? I almost drool remembering that meal.
> *Check.*
> Find a cute European guy for Lisa? *Uh... I guess
> check?*

I turn to Day 3.

> Day 3:
> Sit on the Spanish Steps and make up backstories
> for the people around us.
> Have Lisa throw three coins into the Trevi Foun-
> tain.
> Meet up with the cute guy from yesterday.
> Whatever else Lisa wants to do!

I drop my face into my hand. Apparently I executed my mom's itinerary all wrong. Part of me enjoys doing this "one day at a time" approach, like a little daily surprise from my mom, but little did I know I knocked out two of today's items already. Also, there is no chance in hell I'm going to seek out Luc again. I cringe at remembering the feeling of his hand on my thigh.

Back to yesterday's plans—I should hit up one of the older sites. The Trevi Fountain is old, sure, but it's not *Roman Empire* old. The breeze coming in through the open window is telling me I want to be indoors, but the thing about old stuff is that their roofs are gone. I take a deep breath and hoist myself off the bed. If I don't leave now, I'll be out there in the hottest part of the day.

I go down to reception and ask about how to get to the Colosseum. There's an option to bus, but I have a feeling that the confined space and odor will not be kind to my rolling stomach. Walking might be the best avenue. Once I step out onto the street into the sticky, muggy air, however, I realize I waited far too long to do anything outdoors today.

The receptionist initially laughs at my change of heart before giving me directions to the Vatican. Without prompting, she also points out a pharmacy where I can get a Gatorade on the way.

Ice-cold sports drink in hand and blisters bandaged, I walk for about half an hour to the Vatican. By the time I get there, the midday sun is baking my hair and I am missing the baseball cap I packed in my suitcase. Security lines look short. Too short. Almost non-existent...

Oh, shit. It's Sunday.

I reach into my bag and pull out my guidebook. Good ol' Bob has it right on the top of his Vatican page: Closed on Sundays. My groan startles an elderly couple walking by.

This is a fucking mess. This trip is a mess. I try to do this one last thing for my mom and it is an absolute *mess*. I walk to let off the steam, ending up back on a bridge over the Tiber. A light breeze coming down the river hits the sweat in my hairline *just* right, so I pause to look out over water. It's a murky green, definitely not something you want to swim in, but the color compliments the trees along the shore and accents the orange of the buildings nearby. The next bridge over is absolutely gorgeous and leads to a cylindrical structure. An *old* cylindrical structure with a *roof*. A quick detour takes me over that bridge, past some guys dressed up as Roman soldiers asking if I want to take pictures with them, and into the outer walls.

Upon entering the ticket line, I snag a brochure in English. It is the Castel Sant'Angelo, originally built in the 2nd century, as was clear from the aged rock forming the wall to my right. The pictures show some updated living spaces, art, and some older fortifications. I guess we're living by impulse again. I buy my ticket and make my way around the entire perimeter before coming to the entrance to the building itself—a staircase down into dark and cool, albeit stagnant, air.

High arches amplify the sound of children running up the long, winding hallway before I take a ramp to an open courtyard. While I'm not thrilled to be thrust back into the bright sunlight just yet, I get a stunning view of the city from this vantage point, as well as many others as I circle the building. An unassuming door leads me to an ornately decorated room with paintings on every surface but the floor. I suppose I didn't have to go to the Sistine Chapel to crane my neck to see great works of art commissioned by a pope. I take my time in these papal rooms, enjoying the quiet and relative dark.

I spend a good few hours looking at this building that served many purposes over the years, pleasantly surprised by this mausoleum that I completely glossed over while looking at my mom's guidebook.

I find more stairs that will take me to the top of the wall surrounding the building, and I consider climbing them for even better views of Rome. Instead I return to an outdoor space that has some cafe tables under arches. I grab a soda from the little shop and manage to snag a seat with a beautiful view and a pleasant breeze. I alternate between looking out over the vista and watching people walking by on their own tours. At one point, my eyes are drawn toward where I hear laughter and I see—no. It couldn't be. *But it is.* He has a notebook out and is asking questions to an employee. He pats the guide on the shoulder and continues my way.

Do I say hi? Do I turn away and pretend I never saw him? What is the etiquette here?

Before I can fully consider my options, his name comes spilling out of my mouth. "Rocky!"

His brow furrows before he finally spots me and I swear his face lights up. "Lisa?" He points to the empty seat across from me. After I nod, he plops down onto it with a long sigh. "Romans love their stairs. What are you doing here?"

I shrug. "The tourist thing, I guess."

He takes off his backpack and shoves his notebook inside. "I didn't really peg you as a mausoleum girl, though."

"What? Did you think I was a bar crawl girl?"

He laughs. "Most definitely not. You did not seem to be enjoying yourself as much as other participants were."

I roll my eyes. "I *was* going to be a Vatican girl today, but..."

He clicks his tongue. "Sunday."

"Sunday," I repeat before taking a long sip of my beverage. "So does this mean you're a mausoleum boy?"

He considers this for a moment before responding, his words starting slowly. "I... I try to do as much as I can when I'm abroad. But honestly, I come here specifically because... Eh... Never mind, it sounds stupid."

My face loses all humor. "As stupid as walking all the way to the Vatican, with a hangover, in the same shoes you've been wearing for three days, only to realize it's closed when you try to find the security line?" I'm not sure how I am already so comfortable with Rocky. I don't open up easily. Maybe it's because this man looks *so damn familiar*. I'm going to figure it out. Probably after I leave Rome and I'll never see him again, though.

He holds up his hands in surrender. "Fine. I like to walk the ramparts and pretend I'm an assassin."

I stare at him for a second, waiting to see if he's being serious. He gives me nothing, so I clarify. "An assassin?"

He scrunches his face. "I told you it sounds stupid! It's from a game I played as a kid. It wasn't even my game—my dad would have killed me if he knew I was playing a Rated M game when I was, what, 10? Anyway, you're an assassin, and part of the game happens here."

I can't help but laugh. "Assassin's Creed?"

He nods, his cheeks rosy with embarrassment. "Brotherhood, to be specific."

I lean in close, elbows on the table. "You didn't actually kill anyone up there, did you?"

He mirrors my conspiratorial pose, his eyes serious, his face inches from mine, and whispers, "Absolutely...not. I did say *pretend*, right?" He leans back in his chair. "Enough about appeasing my inner child. Are you going to the Vatican tomorrow? I'd love to accidentally bump into you there."

"Unfortunately, no. I leave tomorrow morning."

"What a shame, coming all the way to Rome and not getting to see the Vatican. You at least got to see the Colosseum, right?"

I shake my head the tiniest bit.

"Seriously? At the very least you threw one coin in the Trevi Fountain." He stares at me as if my response determines whether or not he will ever speak to me again.

"I threw two...and a half. Why just one?"

"Because if you throw in one coin it means you'll return to... Wait. How do you throw *half* a coin?"

"It wasn't my coin—someone else threw it, missed, and I helped it into the fountain."

"Does that count?"

"I don't know. That's why I called it a half." My cheeks hurt from smiling at this point and, again, I do something impulsive. "Do you want to go to dinner?"

I wasn't sure what his reaction would be, but the pleasant surprise on his face was one of the better possible outcomes. "Yes. I would love to."

I thought I couldn't smile any wider, but here we are. "I haven't really looked into where to eat yet—" I reach into my bag and pull out my *Bob Adams,* "—but this probably has some good suggestions."

Rocky reaches across the table and takes the book from me. "As much as I love Bob-O, he is not needed tonight." He tosses the book and it lands back in my bag. "I know a place."

Chapter 5

We walk side-by-side back across the river and down a few cob-blestone streets. As we venture further from touristy areas, the signage contains less and less English, and I start to become more and more aware that I am accompanied by a stranger in a foreign city. I take out my phone and text my sister.

Lisa: Hey, I'm on a date? I think? Turning on my location in case you don't hear from me.

We're not even a block further before I get a response.

Alice: WHAT?! I mean, go out and get some, you deserve it, but maybe don't get murdered and leave me an orphan AND an only child?
Lisa: Your fault for not coming on the trip. Love you!
Alice: If you end up at a hotel that's not yours, I'm calling the policios, or whatever the cops in Italy are called.

Lisa: Restaurant, then hotel. I'll text you if the
plan changes.
Alice: Is he cute?
Lisa: Yeah, he's cute. Looks really familiar,
though, but I can't place it.
Alice: American?
Lisa: Yep.
Lisa: I think.
Lisa: Maybe Canadian? He might be too nice to
be American.
Alice: Name?
Lisa: Rocky.
Alice: Like the squirrel?

I laugh to myself but don't respond. I should really be more
present as we wind down alleys to this mystery restaurant. It
isn't long before we arrive, which is good because my feet are
screaming at me.

The restaurant is a tiny thing with four little tables outside
and a handful of four-tops squeezed into the building itself.

The middle-aged woman filling up wine glasses spots us and
does a double-take. "Pietro! Benvenuto!" She excuses herself
from the table she's helping and wraps Rocky in an embrace.
Her attention turns to me. "And you bring a girl!" Suddenly
I'm wrapped in her warm arms, my body stiff, unsure what to
do. She pulls away and looks me up and down. "Pietro always
comes alone, every year. This year, he brings a girl. Wonderful!"

She leads us to an outdoor table and disappears back into the
restaurant, bouncing like a proud mother.

"Pietro?" I ask.

"Stone in Italian," he explains, settling into his chair. "Carlotta had a really hard time with my name, so we came to that compromise."

"And you come here every year?"

"For the past—" he puffs out his cheeks while he calculates, "—four years. My work brings me to Rome annually, hence why I'm usually here alone. I was introduced to this place on my first trip, so I like to come back to visit."

"What do you do for work?"

"I work in publishing, editing mostly—"

We are interrupted when Carlotta comes back with a bottle of wine and a bottle of water—flat, thankfully. She starts speaking to Rocky in her own language, and he laughs and nods, responding in what seems to be slightly slower, but still confident Italian.

He turns to me. "She wants to make me the things I usually get. Is that alright with you?"

Normally I'd look up everything on the menu on Google to make sure I wasn't getting in too far over my head culinarily, but this sounds kind of fun. Plus, worst-case scenario, I eat nothing and gorge myself on gelato on the walk back to the hotel. "Sure, sounds good to me."

"Any allergies?"

"No. None." I glance at the bottle of wine on the table. "Actually, wine does make me break out in hives sometimes, so maybe I could get something else to drink?"

Rocky relays my request, causing Carlotta to stare at me like I have three heads. Once it seems the shock has worn off, she gives Rocky a warm smile before walking back into the kitchen.

"I mean, I *can* drink it," I explain in a hushed tone. "I just get really itchy."

Rocky shakes his head. "Carlotta will be fine. She'll find you something else. But, wine? Really?"

I shrug. "It's just on my chest. Sometimes it's worth it, but with the heat and the sweating, it would be pretty uncomfortable."

Carlotta brings out a red-orange drink, garnished with an orange, as well as a plate of fried something. I taste my drink—a lot more bitter than I expected, but overall it's pretty good. Some kind of liquor and soda water. The appetizer smells *amazing*. Rocky breaks one open to reveal rice and tomato sauce and a gooey, cheesy center. The surprise dinner was the right choice.

Rocky finishes his first and grabs a second fried rice ball. "You never shared what you do for work."

I finagle the thread of melted cheese connecting my lips to the plate with the grace of a beached whale before I finally respond. "Instructional design. I went to school for teaching, then when I started student teaching I realized it was not for me, but I was already three years into the program and wasn't about to start over. Thank goodness I figured out something else to do with that degree."

"You don't like kids?" he asks with a smile.

"I like kids fine. I have two nephews who I adore. It's thirty kids leaving thirty kids' worth of mess and making thirty kids' worth of noise that I had trouble with." I scoot my glass a few centimeters closer to my plate. "I prefer feeling like I'm in control of my environment."

"So traveling must be going great for you." The sarcasm drips off his words.

My eyes go wide. "They lost my bag. They sent it to Florida." I gesture to myself. "This is the shirt I wore on the plane and then washed in my bathroom sink and hung over a shower curtain rod that has more than likely never been cleaned. Same with the underwear. I could have re-worn my flying jeans, too, but it's balls hot out, so I went with the shorts that are still kind of sticky from getting alcohol spilled on them last night." I stick my foot out from under the table, showing him my ankle boots. "These are the shoes that wouldn't fit in my checked bag, so I wore them on the plane. They are most definitely *not* good walking shoes, but I can't go shopping because one, the stores are all closed and two, if I buy more shoes I won't be able to carry them around because there is no room in my bags." Wow, I really needed to vent to someone about this, and apparently I am not done yet. "And I didn't even really want to take this trip. My mom said I needed to go out and *have an adventure*, but she was supposed to be here with me but she died a few weeks ago and I am supposed to be grieving, but here I am trying to figure out what to do *alone* in a foreign country." I finally fill my lungs to recover from that word vomit of a sentence, only to realize that I am taking heaving mid-sob breaths.

Carlotta arrives again and, upon seeing my tears, asks Rocky, "Should I wait?"

Rocky shakes his head and guides the two plates of food onto the table. "No, we might need this." He pushes one of the plates in front of me. "It's no Ben and Jerry's, but pasta helps. Now, do you want to talk about it or be distracted from it?"

I take a whiff of the food in front of me. If any food is going to give me the strength to open up about this, it is pasta. *And maybe some of this.* I take a sip of my drink. "I might want to talk about it. Is that alright?"

"I wouldn't have offered it if it wasn't." He pours himself another glass of wine and sits back. "Why didn't you cancel the trip?"

"My mom made everything non-refundable, I think on purpose. I know I could have called the places and told them the situation, but then the money would go back on the credit cards that we already canceled because, you know...she's dead." My voice catches on the last word, so I take a bite of pasta to clear my throat. "Plus, when she was booking everything, she kept saying that we had to go no matter what, that I needed this." I take a sip of my drink. "She thinks I'm wound too tight... Thought. She *thought* I was wound too tight. Am wound?" I trail off.

"Don't worry about tenses. Just get it all out." Rocky takes a few bites of his meal, then leans back again with his glass of wine, giving me his undivided attention.

"I don't know if I'm actually wound too tight; I just like knowing what is going to happen from day to day. That's not weird, it's totally normal. I like routine, I like having familiar people around me." I look at him and narrow my eyes. "And even though I just met you, I swear I know you from somewhere."

"I would know if I'd met you before, but we can go through the whole song and dance so I can convince you that I just have one of those faces." He sits up straight. "Have you ever been to Chicago?"

I shake my head instead of responding since my mouth is full of noodles.

"Did you study abroad in college?"

Again, no.

"Have you been to Europe at all?"

I take a sip of my drink and respond verbally this time. "No. Did you ever live anywhere besides Chicago?"

It's his turn to shake his head. "My whole life was either spent in Chicago or here in Europe."

"Did you play a sport or something in college? Maybe traveled with the team and we met in passing?"

He nearly spits out his wine. "I was playing assassin on a castle wall and you think I was the type to be good enough at sports to play in college?"

I shrug. "You never know. But fine, I've never met you before." While the logical part of my brain conceded, a small piece held onto the idea that he looks familiar. "But maybe I met your identical twin?"

"I don't have a twin, only younger siblings, but good try."

We spend the rest of the pasta course talking about my parents, what they did, and how much I miss them. It is nice to finally open up to someone. Maybe Alice was onto something when she suggested I go to therapy. This is cheaper, though, and a whole lot more delicious. Plus, how long would it take to find a therapist with a smile like Rocky's?

Carlotta comes to take our plates, and I set my napkin on the table. Rocky gives me a questioning look. "Did you not want the next course?"

I light up. *Oh my gosh, she makes desserts, too.* I place my napkin back in my lap as Carlotta arrives with...meat dishes? "There's more?"

"After a good unloading session, you should have some protein for strength, right?" He surveys the food. "Chicken or veal?"

I go for the chicken, having never had veal in my life and not really wanting to start now. The dish is a little oily but still pretty good. I can barely eat half, though, having filled up on pasta. Rocky trades me for his empty plate and finishes the chicken for me.

The conversation never hits a lull, as we discuss Rome and all of his favorite things to do here. It makes me want to come back one day, but we'll see if that ever happens.

As we finish our drinks, my phone vibrates.

Alice: You alive?

"Sorry, I have to respond. It's my sister. She wants to make sure you didn't murder me."

He gives the 'go ahead' gesture and kills his glass of wine.

Lisa: Yeah. Having a really nice night.
Alice: You ever find out his real name?

I start to text "It's Rocky," but pause, looking up at my companion. "Is Rocky your actual name?"

"It's what everyone calls me, even my parents." He gestures to the kitchen. "Everyone except Carlotta, that is."

I narrow my eyes. "But, like, what's on your birth certificate?"

"Robert, but I'm a junior, so I don't get to use that one."

Lisa: It's Robert.
Alice: Yeah, Rocky is a better choice.

I put my phone down on the table, which is illuminated by the flicker of an oil candle. Dark had fallen without me even noticing. "It's getting late. I should probably get back to my hotel."

Rocky stands. "Can I walk you back?"

I stand, a little startled when he helps me with my chair. "I hope so. I have no idea where we are or how to get back without being glued to the GPS on my phone."

He strolls over to settle up with Carlotta. I hear her tell him, "She is pretty. Not Italian, but pretty. Bring her again next year." I don't catch what he says, though, as her arms engulf him in a hug as he tries to respond.

We meander down more streets, and at one point he has to check his own phone to be sure he knows where he is going. I guess he doesn't have the whole city memorized. At some points, our hands dangle close enough to each other that I am tempted to reach out and hold his, but the more tired I get, the less daring I feel.

We finally hit a familiar street and I know we are approaching my hotel.

"So, where are you off to next?" Rocky asks. "Since your bag still isn't here, I assume you're still at the start of your trip."

"Florence. I think I'm going to spend the train ride planning out exactly what I'm going to do for my one day there so I don't get caught going somewhere that's closed. Again."

We stop in the doorway to my hotel. "Can I give you a phone number?" he asks.

I am hit by a twinge of sadness. "I'm not sure what good that will do. I mean, I don't think we'll ever see each other again."

He laughs but with an almost disappointed spin to it. "Not mine, a friend in Florence. He loves showing people around his city. Maybe he can keep you company so you're not alone in Italy again."

"Oh..." Why am I so sad that he wasn't going to offer *his* number? I wasn't even going to take it anyway. He is truly helping me out here. "Yeah, that would be great." I hand him my phone and he inputs a number for "Andrea."

"He works mornings but is usually free in the evenings. His girlfriend is really nice, too. Maybe you could all meet up together for dinner or something."

"Thanks. This is really nice of you." I'm not sure I will actually call, but it's nice to have the option if I need it. I hesitate with the next words, not completely sure I'm reading the vibe right. "Did you want to come up?"

He looks over my shoulder into the hotel. "That is so incredibly tempting, but I think I will have to pass. As you said, we probably won't ever see each other again." He looks deep into my eyes and holds my hand. "I would love a kiss for the road, though, if it's not too much to ask."

"Yeah, that would—" I can't finish my sentence because his lips are already on mine. The kiss is gentle, sincere, and over too soon. I do that stupid lean forward, trying to let our lips linger a bit longer, almost falling off the step I'm on.

"Goodnight, Lisa."

"Goodnight, Rocky. Thank you for...everything."

He gives me a warm smile before walking off into the lamplight of the street.

I float back to my room, not even noticing the absolute pain my feet are in. I lay down in bed, and am almost asleep when my phone vibrates.

Alice: You guys fuck?

Chapter 6

I leave for the train station before the city gets bustling, meaning traffic is a lot better than I was expecting, allowing me to stop for a quick breakfast at a bakery before heading into the terminal itself. It feels weird traveling between two places without giving myself two hours for a security line, but then again, we don't really have extensive trains on the West Coast. Rail travel is relatively new to me. After a bit of a panic when I don't see Florence on the reader board, a helpful staff member informs me that I am looking for Firenze and before long I am on a bright red-orange train, zooming to Tuscany. I take out my trusty *Bob Adams* and a piece of scrap paper I got from my hotel room. Time to make a plan.

I stare at the pages for a half hour, bouncing between "this sounds amazing" and "is it actually worth it if I only have one day there?" for each landmark and museum. In my frustration, I grab my phone.

Lisa: Hi, my name is Lisa. Rocky gave me your number since I'll be in Florence. Is there anything you think I shouldn't miss?

I set my phone down and stare out the window. Farms, orchards, and vineyards with orange-roofed towns scattered in between pass me by. I sip my water, finally feeling adequately hydrated for the first time this entire trip. My phone buzzes.

Andrea: I have been waiting for your message! Rocky tells me you have one day. Choose a museum for the morning, get your ticket now on your phone. I can meet you after work at 13h.

Part of me hesitates. Another strange guy in a foreign place. But Rocky vouched for him, so he can't be horrible, right?

I look up museum tickets on my phone. The Accademia is already sold out for the morning, but the Uffizi Gallery has one ticket left for an 11 am entry, which is perfect because I am exactly one person. I buy the ticket and send off another text.

Lisa: That sounds great. I'll be at the Uffizi Gallery.

I put my phone away, my hand bumping against my mom's itinerary. Let's see what she has to say about today.

Day 4:
Early train to Florence (Firenze)
See a big, naked rock man
WINE (not for Lisa)
Sunset at Piazzale Michelangelo

Sorry, Mom. No David for me this trip. Though, I suppose there will be plenty of naked statues at this other museum, too.

I take another car from the train station to my hotel. I try to memorize the streets as we get closer, but it looks like most of the buildings were made at the same time, in the same style, using the same color scheme. It makes for a great overall aesthetic, but a horrible way to figure out where you are.

It's too early to get my room, but I decide to check in, anyway. Besides, I can drop my carry-on at the front desk and not have to worry about bag size restrictions wherever I end up going. I fling my bag onto the receptionist's desk and I see it. Purple, beautiful, a little dented, but I don't care because *my bag is here.*

"Ah, you must be Elisabeth! This bag arrived just before you." The receptionist must have noticed the longing in my eyes because she quickly rolls my suitcase over to me. "If you want, you can use the restroom down the hall to freshen up and change."

I don't even bother to extend the handle, instead hunching over my bag to roll it to the back. There is something special about the joy you feel when you know you can finally get some clean underwear and a bra you haven't been sweating in for three days in a row. I also pull out some more comfortable walking shoes and a sundress, then cram everything back in—not an easy task in that tiny restroom. Once I'm moderately put together, I make my way back to the receptionist's desk.

The woman is typing away at the computer with a smile. "While you were changing, I went ahead and checked you in. I only need a card and your identification, and your room will be ready for you this afternoon, say around 3:00?"

I give her my cards and roll the suitcase back around the desk.

"Perfetto!" She hands me back my cards. "Can I give you directions anywhere?"

"Yeah, the Uffizi Gallery." I glance at the time on my phone. "Can I walk there in less than an hour?"

She takes out a map and lays it between us. "Fifteen minutes to walk. You have plenty of time." She points out a few routes I might want to take, and I choose the one along the river since I have the time.

Once again, the river is a city river—not quite the blue hue one would normally associate with a body of water. Still, the view of the opposite bank and bridges is lovely as I find my way to the courtyard that will bring me to the gallery. The overall bustle of the city is tamer than Rome, but still present as I bob and weave through tourists and locals alike. The timed entry ticket gets me in fairly quickly—not exactly at 11, but close enough.

Unlike at Castel Sant'Angelo, the art is not part of the building. In the first exhibits, the rooms themselves are blank white, only a backdrop upon which the art is featured. Part of it feels stale, but when I dive into the artwork itself, I appreciate the room not distracting me from the detail and color. It isn't long before I find my first "big, naked rock man" and I mentally check that off my mom's list. I'm not sure how big David is, but I can only assume that these gentlemen measure up. *Not like that.*

I see the big ticket paintings, a.k.a. the ones in an additional protective plexiglass frame: The Birth of Venus, Primavera, Medusa. I even see a Della Francesca, whose name I only know because my mom and I binge-watched Downton Abbey after Dad died. I have the urge to share this tidbit with my mom, and I pull out my phone only to realize... I can't.

What hurts more than realizing she isn't here anymore is the moment that I thought she was; that there is a version of me that doesn't miss my mom because she doesn't know she is gone, and this version is able to enjoy an art museum without feeling like a key part of her is missing.

I shake off my weird psychological "ignorance is bliss" thing and wipe my tears with the back of my hand.

An old woman who is also admiring the picture hands me a tissue. "Is beautiful, yes?"

I take the tissue and dry off what's left on my cheeks. Not wanting to go into detail about me and my dead mom's watch-through of a British period drama bringing me to tears, I force a smile and nod.

After a trip to the bathroom to blow my nose, I walk through a few more galleries. Some pieces I walk by without a second thought, while others draw me in, making me lose track of time as I get lost in the figures, the colors, or the story.

Right at one, my phone buzzes. Multiple times. Oh my gosh, it's a call. Who the hell calls people these days? Either some politician wants my money, someone wants to contact me about my car's extended warranty, or someone else in my family died. I breathe a sigh of relief when I see Andrea's name. I scurry out of the room and find a stairway.

"Hello?"

"Lisa! It is Andrea, Rocky's friend. I am here at the Uffizi."

"Hi! Let me get outside real quick." My feet don't move right away. I have to take a second to convince myself that this isn't about to be a *Taken* scenario. *It's a very public space. It's fine.* I scurry down the stairs and find an exit, which brings me back into the courtyard. I pivot, looking for people on their phones. There are at least a dozen of them. "I'm here. There's a guy selling paintings right in front of me. I'm in a blue dress."

A young man on a phone turns around and makes eye contact. When one has daydreams about falling madly in love in Italy, this man is close to what they would picture. Dark hair, muscular, strong jaw, and a thick five o'clock shadow that you kind of want to see him grow out. With a smile, I see his lips move and then hear his voice milliseconds later. "I see you."

I meet him halfway and he holds out his hand, pulling me in for a kiss on each cheek once I take it. "So what are we doing for your one day in Firenze?"

"I don't know what *to* do." I gesture to the door I just left from. "I think I'm good on art for the day, though. Oh, and—" I pull my mom's itinerary out of my purse, "—I need to watch the sunset here." I point to the words "Piazzale Michelangelo."

"That is perfect. My girlfriend works near there. We can all get dinner together and watch the sunset. I hope it is alright if she joins us?"

"Yeah, absolutely." Honestly, I think I prefer it.

"But first, lunch. Have you eaten yet?"

I check in with myself. The feeling of fullness from last night's dinner is finally wearing off. "Lunch sounds great. Maybe nothing too heavy if we're going to do a big meal tonight."

His lips morph into a mischievous smile. "I know just the thing." He leads me a few streets over to a small little hole in the wall, from which wafts the smell of fried dough. "When in Florence, you try coccoli." He orders in Italian, turning back to me at one point to ask, "You eat meat, yes?"

"Yeah, I'll try anything."

He finishes the order and we wait at a table. "But no wine. Rocky told me you don't drink wine, so a tour of wine country was not an option. Such a travesty."

"It still might have been nice to see the vineyards, but no, I wouldn't enjoy it as much as other people might."

"Then what do you think of a walking tour? I can take you around, show you where everything is? I have an appointment at four, so I will have to leave you for a while, but we can meet again for the sunset dinner."

"That sounds perfect! I wore my walking shoes today, so I am ready to go!" It sounds stupid when it comes out of my mouth, but I am just so excited to *finally* have proper footwear.

A person behind the counter hails Andrea, and he pops away for a minute, coming back with balls of fried dough. He breaks one open to show it is stuffed with meat and oozing with cheese. Once again, I am overwhelmed with the incredible deliciousness of Italian food. I mean, fried dough is always good, and cheese is always good, but this combination is really hitting the spot right now.

It is a light lunch in volume, but the grease leaves me feeling pretty full and ready to walk off those calories. Andrea guides me back to the gallery, then straight down a pedestrian road that starts and ends with Renaissance beauty.

We start at a piazza with a large clock tower. Right at the base are more naked men made of stone—including David himself. Well, a copy of David. Still, I snap a picture and quickly send it to my sister.

"Did you want me to take a picture of you with him?" Andrea asks.

"Oh my God." I start to hand him my phone, then freeze. "I haven't taken any pictures of myself yet. I was in Rome and have no pictures of myself there to prove it. There are *no* pictures of me in Rome."

"Well, let's not let that happen here." He takes it from me and scoots back a few steps. "Uno, due, tre!"

I pose, fighting the voice in the back of my head that is telling me that smiling right now isn't appropriate—that sharing this picture with anyone will just show them I am not sad about my parents' deaths. *No.* My mom would want me to enjoy myself. She would want me to have ways to look back at this as a positive experience. I get my phone back, survey the picture, and send it to my sister. She'll call me out if the smile is inappropriate. I hand the phone back to Andrea and ask, "Can you get me in front of the palace, too?"

Andrea holds the phone out in front of him, looks confused for a few beats, then seems to collapse to the floor.

I rush over to help him, only to find that he is doubled over laughing. When I ask what is so funny, he hands me my phone back, text notification on the top of the screen.

Alice: Is that "Rocky?" Hopefully a grower, not
a shower.

My hand covers my mouth as I fight a rising blush. Andrea is still trying to recover his breath. Leave it to my sister to lighten the mood in the most inappropriate way.

We continue our walk, Andrea leading me past a church and dozens of shops. People around us are weighed down with multiple shopping bags, some from fairly high-end stores. Not noticing anything particularly note-worthy in the "walking tour" department, I decide to get to know about more than just the city.

"How do you know Rocky?"

A smile stretches across Andrea's face, one that hints that those two have gotten into a lot of trouble before. "He spent a semester here when he was in university, and that's how we became so close. But we actually met when we were children. He came here with his family when he was ten. They went to a park to play and he joined a football match with me and my friends. He was *terrible*, but he had a good mood about it. I am sure he never played before that day. Or watched a match."

"Did you two keep in touch in between being kids and college?"

"I think we tried to write letters for a few years, but it did not last. It did help me learn more English, though."

"Did he tell you he was studying in Florence?"

"No. He saw me at a bar and recognized me." He pauses for a nostalgic chuckle. "I was confused because he says he is the little American kid from the football match, but he says it in very good italiano."

I cock my head to the side. "Aww, that would make a really cute romantic comedy."

He shakes his head. "Not as cute as running into the man who helped you home from a bar crawl at a castle cafe."

My jaw drops. "How much did he tell you?"

"When he asks me to show someone around my city, I usually ask who the person is. He couldn't even give me your last name, so I needed to know the story."

"I guess that's fair." A bright dessert catches my eye and I slow to get a better look, deciding if I can overcome the temptation, but Andrea pulls me along.

"You do not want that. Real lemons are not yellow. Well, they are yellow, but not—" he points to a bright yellow tub of gelato, "—*yellow*."

My curiosity quickly squashes my disappointment when I see another piazza coming up—and it's a big one. It's *the* big one. When we step out from between the tall buildings that create the pedestrian road, I spot a huge bell tower alongside the red-capped Duomo.

Andrea looks at his watch. "I will get one picture of you here, then I have to go. The Duomo is free to enter if you would like to see it. Sofia ends work at six in the evening, but sometimes she takes a long time to say goodbye, so we can meet you at the Piazzale at seven?"

I look at my watch—3:00. This gives me just enough time to do a little exploring, then go lay down for a spell. "Perfect. I'll text you when I'm on my way."

We get a few shots of me in front of the beautiful Renaissance cathedral, and then upon my request, Andrea joins me for a selfie. He leaves with an air kiss on each of my cheeks. Even after he leaves, although I know I'm alone in this city, I don't feel *lonely*.

There is a short wait to get into the cathedral. The rest of the Duomo is ticketed, but I am content just going into the main space; it's not like I have the whole day left to explore. As I enter, I immediately crane my neck, expecting some beautiful painted ceiling, but disappointment hits when I realize it isn't decorated at all. There are some paintings and statues here and there, but I expected a lot more based on the grandeur of the outside. I move from pillar to pillar, taking in the architecture, then find my way to the altar placed far inside. As I approach, it is almost like the dull murmurs from the groups around me fall away. My heartbeat thumps quietly in my head as my eyes are once more drawn upwards, but this time it is not disappointment, but rather calm that fills me.

The scene above is of people standing on the clouds, joyous in heaven, light streaming in from the top of the dome in the center. I never held much belief in the afterlife, but in this moment I hope my parents are in a place like that—that my dad is no longer in pain and my mom is happy.

My breath catches when I see her—a woman in white and orange, her face serene and familiar. It could have been modeled on my mother in her youth. I am shocked by the fact I am not crying. It's as if this new found stillness inside me won't allow for tears. I sneakily take a picture with my phone, not remembering whether or not photography is allowed, and exit the church.

As I walk back to my hotel, I send the picture to my sister.

Lisa: Does this look like Mom to you?
Alice: A little? I guess?

What does she mean *a little*? It was her spitting image. It looked more like her than Alice or I do. I glance at the picture again. Upon second look, maybe Alice is right. It's not really that close. I swear it looked *just* like her when I was inside.

Alice: I've been seeing her places, too.

Once I meander back to the hotel, the front desk gives me my key, telling me my bags are already in my room. Bags. Plural. Oh, isn't that nice to hear? Once I get inside, I fall onto the bed, letting my feet dangle off the side because I am too tired to even take off my shoes.

When I wake up, I take a rideshare to meet Andrea and Sofia. She is absolutely lovely—the pair of them are like a couple in those ethereal perfume ads. She doesn't speak much English, though, so we stick to pretty superficial conversations unless Andrea is ready to act as translator.

We get dinner and I do a much better job at pacing myself, not downing the entire pasta dish so I can leave room for some much-needed protein. The meal isn't quite as good as Carlotta's, but the view from this restaurant could not be beat. The piazzale is on a hill overlooking Florence, the red cap of the Duomo peeking out over the labyrinth of buildings. The western-facing walls glow in the light of the setting sun, warming the city in a way the midday heat could not. We sip Negronis until dark when Sofia and Andrea have to leave. We kiss on the cheek and I thank them for a wonderful time, but I remain for a while, watching the lights turn on all around the city, before heading back to my hotel.

When I step out of the shower, I see red blotches on my chest in the mirror. A quick internet search informs me that the Negroni includes fortified wine, so that's fun. I spread lotion all over my chest before heading to sleep, hopefully taming the reaction before it fully develops. I guess I did complete my mom's list after all, wine included.

Chapter 7

Another early morning has me out of the hotel before the complimentary breakfast even has a chance to start. The smell as I walk into the street gives me pause. I know that smell. The sections of my brain still at rest finally boot up and it hits me—rain. It rained last night. Not much, but enough for the slightly moist ground to give off that distinctive scent. I have a faint smile on my lips as I make my way to the train station.

Navigating the platform with the crowd of people getting off another train is even more difficult with my rolling suitcase in tow. It keeps getting caught as I try to hop back and forth over the raised lines and bumps on the ground. On the umpteenth time I try to free it, I lurch forward, throwing my body into a passerby.

"I am so sorry, I—" I push the hair out of my face and look upon the person I just accidentally assaulted. "No fucking way."

Rocky's shock quickly shifts into a laugh as he shakes his head. "No. Fucking. Way."

"You didn't tell me you were coming to Florence." I look around, trying to find a space to tuck off into in order to get out of the way, but there is nowhere. People just flow around us instead.

"I didn't think it would matter since you were leaving today."

"Still, Andrea should have said something." I peek at the sign above his head. It's still a few more minutes until my train arrives.

"Andrea doesn't know. I'm going to surprise him at work."

"You two really have that bromance thing down. He gushes about you."

"I'll pretend you didn't say that when we're drinking beer and watching sports together tonight." He looks up at the signage. "Venice? Want any tips?"

"Oh, so you've been to Venice, too? Quite the traveler."

"I've been a few times, yeah. I studied abroad here; it was a fun weekend trip."

The rush of people finally dies down, so I take Rocky's wrist and pull him closer to the middle of the platform behind a post so we're more out of the way. "Sure, what are your tips?"

"How many days are you there?"

"Just two." I shrug.

A sort of smug expression flashes across his face, but it's so quick I hardly catch it. "Alright, so I'd say today you should check out Doge's Palace if you can get tickets. If not, still go see the Basilica and Piazza San Marco. For day two, I would just explore the city, walk around, get lost, but make sure to end up right in the middle of the Academy Bridge at noon."

My train starts to pull in, causing me to have to raise my voice over the growing chaos. "What happens at noon?"

"Oh, you'll see. Also, skip the gondolas. Those are just tourist traps."

"Really?" I ask, knowing almost for certain my mom is going to have it on her itinerary.

"Absolutely. Maybe if you *need* to do it, save it for the last evening. That way if you're disappointed it won't ruin the vibe for the rest of the visit." An automated voice comes over the speakers announcing the train's arrival. Rocky looks over my shoulder at the red-striped locomotive. "Your carriage awaits."

I stare at him. More specifically, I stare at his lips, remembering the last time we saw each other. *Man, his lips look soft. I mean, they are soft, but maybe I should kiss him again just to see if I remember correctly.* A dinging from inside the train snaps me out of it. "Yeah, I should go." I exert way too much effort trying to get my bag facing the right direction before I go. "Tell Andrea I say hello, and thank him again for me. It was nice to have someone to show me around. You wouldn't happen to have a friend in Venice, would you?"

He shakes his head. "I'm afraid not."

I shrug as I walk away. "It was worth a shot. San Marco today, explore tomorrow, bridge at noon, no gondolas. Got it!"

He shouts after me, "*Academy* Bridge!"

"Academy Bridge!" I repeat, hoisting my bag onto the train.

I store my luggage and find my seat. It feels weird to be so far away from my suitcase, but at least my seat has a good view of the luggage rack. I mean, I'm not sure just what I would do if someone came and walked it off the train—chase after them and risk getting stuck in whatever city we're stopped in? Either way, I have some false sense of security in that at least I will know *when* my bag gets stolen.

As we pull away, I look out my window to see Rocky still standing there, waving goodbye. I wave back, kicking myself for not getting his phone number. Even if whatever romance I've concocted in my head is doomed from the start, it would still be useful to have his advice moving forward in my trip.

I shimmy into my seat and pull out my mom's itinerary.

Day 5:
Early train to Venice
Vaporetto to hotel (2, S. Marco stop)
People watch in St. Mark's Square
Enjoy the view
Gondola ride for two!

Well, kind of hard to do that last one, Mom.

I open the *Bob Adams* and thumb through until I find the Doge's Palace. It was the palace of the ruler of Venice back when it governed itself. Lavish, extravagant. Lots of paintings. I'll decide if I want to do it in the moment—if there are any tickets left, that is. For now, my only plan is the Basilica and the people-watching.

I pass the time on the train with a show on my phone, followed by a nap—it is early, after all. Two and a half hours later, I wake up to the announcement declaring that we've arrived. I was hoping to catch views of Venice as we came in, but I guess I will just have to see it on the way out. My bag is still *close* to where I left it—I guess at some point someone decided mine needed to be on a higher shelf. This would be fine if I was taller or had better upper body strength. Or if I'd packed less... A crew member rushes to my side as I am about to lose my balance.

I find the Vaporetto station, following a crowd of people also tugging large suitcases behind them. After a short wait, I make my way onto one of the floating buses. There are no seats available, but I am happy standing along the rail, more than ready to take in the views.

And what views they are. As we motor down the Grand Canal, boat after boat passes us going the opposite direction. Sleek wooden boats, tiny motorboats, other Vaporettos, water taxis, delivery boats, and even a garbage boat. I was so entranced with what was on the water that it took me a while to even notice what was right next to the canal—huge buildings that not only face the water, but come right up to it. You could step off a boat right to their front door. The bright colors reflect off the water and the architecture makes it look like these massive structures are floating on the surface. We go under a few bridges, and I make note when the stop is called Accademia with a large wooden bridge just ahead—that must be the one I am heading to tomorrow. Though, I could just go at noon today to see what's up...

About half an hour later, our Vaporetto is leaving the Grand Canal. I panic, wondering if I missed my stop, but thankfully the boat pulls into the San Marco stop right before I get desperate enough to ask for help. I hop off, hoping to see street signs or some other indicator of how to get around, but there is nothing. I veer off to the side to try to get my bearings. I reach for my phone, but I can't seem to find it buried in my bag, so

I decide to squeeze into the nearest hotel to ask for directions. Maybe they have a map or something I could use.

The hotel right off the Vaporetto stop is unassuming from the outside. It doesn't directly abut the water, only because there is a little patio for their restaurant. The inside, though, gives the impression that it was built for people in a much higher tax bracket than me. Vaulted ceilings, a marble staircase, stone pillars, and that is just the lobby. I walk up to the front desk, where a man in a suit and tie is shuffling some papers. The suit *looks* expensive. Not that I know much about expensive clothes, but it is at the very least well-tailored.

"Excuse me, can you help me find this hotel?" I point to the name on my list of hotels and confirmation numbers for the trip.

"Yes, are you checking in?" The man asks.

I give a small laugh as I turn to scan the lobby once more. "No, I just need directions."

He looks confused for a moment, then it melts into a "bless your heart" smile. "Of course." He points to the doorway. "Go out the doors, turn around, and come back inside."

I look at the name again, then spot the same name on the business card on the counter. *Holy shit. This is my hotel.* My face gets hot as I laugh off my embarrassment. "Then yes, I suppose I am checking in." I rummage through my bag to get my ID and credit card. "I am so sorry—my mom made the reservation. I didn't realize she would book something so nice."

He looks at my ID and types it into his computer. "Is this under Diana?"

"Diane, yes. She is not on this trip, though. Just me."

He looks up, scanning my face. "I am sorry she could not make it."

I want to say something in return, but the lump in my throat makes it difficult. Instead, I give a weak smile as he continues putting in my information.

"Your room will be ready this afternoon. You can leave your bags with the porter and we will have them brought to your room when it is ready. Just come to the desk for your key and room number." He slides me my cards.

I thank him, hand my bag and carry-on over to a uniformed bellhop, and stroll outside, veering back toward the Vaporetto stop, looking for a sign for St. Mark's Square. Instead, I see a tour group and tag along behind them, not understanding a lick of what the guide is saying, but pretty confident they will lead me to the right place. At the very least lead me somewhere interesting. We walk along the water, some people from the group slowing every so often to look at tacky souvenirs. After taking a bridge over the entrance to a smaller canal and walking alongside a beautiful waterfront park, an immense square opens up on my left.

The tour group makes its way directly to what I assume to be the palace, but my eyes veer upward. The entrance to the square has statues on pillars, but even higher is the bell tower. *Enjoy the view.* My legs are on fire just imagining the stairs up there, but that is what I want to do today: I want to see the view from that bell tower. The line is shorter than the one for the Basilica, so I join it immediately.

While I wait, I take in the other wing of the square—it seems to make an L around this tower. Pigeons are *everywhere*. Kids are either chasing after them or trying to feed them. One little girl manages to get one to land on her wrist and eat out of her hand. And then it shits on her. She runs to her mother, scream-crying.

I scoot forward in line a sizable distance.

As I'm stretching out my calves, I take note of the cafes and restaurants. It seems I have some lunch options with a people-watching view. I just hope a well-fed bird doesn't try to get too friendly while I'm eating.

The line shifts forward more.

I turn around to look at the palace behind me. Like, I get a royal family of a large country living in a place like that, but this guy was in charge of *Venice*. A couple of islands. Probably not that huge of a population. He had to be raking in the taxes to build that. Plus, it's *gorgeous*, and the location is ten out of ten. Imagine what a sale that would be in real estate...

Someone taps my shoulder. The line had moved without me. I shimmy forward, up some steps toward the gorgeous facade with columns and marble statues.

As I enter the doorway, the most incredible sight stands before me. No. Not Rocky. He's in Florence, remember? It's a sign for an *elevator.*

This thing has an elevator! If my legs could sigh with relief, they would. It whisks me and a swarm of other tourists to the top in less than a minute. When I get to a free opening along the railing, I am met with red rooftops that stretch to the sea with great churches peeking out over them. Boats enter the canal, looking like little toys from this height. A child pushes past me, trying to get to the view. His parents say something in their language in an apologetic tone, and I scoot to the side so they can all look together.

The scene is perfect—a breathtaking view of a city that is over a thousand years old. My eyes drop to the family beside me. The mom is now down on the child's level, pointing out places of interest. The boy has his arms wrapped around his mom's neck. Their cheeks are pressed together until he turns to plant a kiss on his mom's.

My nose starts to hurt, so I press my eyes shut to stop whatever waterworks are trying to go off. I move around to the other side of the tower, finding another opening with an incredible view of the rest of the city. I pull out my phone to take pictures, snapping a few before turning around for a selfie. A stranger offers to take one for me, but I decline—not sure a phone thief would practice their craft in a place where the only getaway is an elevator, but I'm not going to risk it.

I soak in the view a little longer, properly enjoying it as my mother would have wanted me to, before heading back to the elevator and down into the square. It got even busier in the time I was up there. The line for the Doge's Palace now goes the entire length of the palace itself. I think I'll pass.

Instead I find a cafe, opting for outside seating despite the temperature creeping up. Bob Adams says not to eat where the menu is translated into English, but I'm going to make an exception here since the location is unbeatable. If I'm going to people-watch properly in this square, you bet I'm going to be eating while I'm doing it.

As I munch on overpriced tea sandwiches and rehydrate with some fizzy orange drink, I start making up backstories like I used to with Mom.

The couple walking up to the cafe, the wife's arms crossed and brow scrunched? He told her that she was cranky because she's hungry, but she's too stubborn to admit he is right.

The middle-aged woman in huge sunglasses, holding her head, trailing behind the rest of her group? That's a hangover if I've ever seen one before. She had a bit too much vino last night and just woke up. *Been there, girl.*

The muscular man being berated by his equally muscular traveling companion? I'm guessing his eyes lingered on a handsome local for a little too long and his boyfriend is *not* having it.

The pregnant woman, sitting in a chair with her feet up on another chair, her husband fanning her with a folded-up map? The husband wanted to surprise her with one last romantic trip before the baby was born but didn't realize how much walking would be involved in a city with no cars, so now he is waiting on her hand and foot to make it up to her.

Despite my early morning, I feel pretty invigorated and am ready to power through the rest of the day. So far I've seen the rest of the city via water, but now I have an urge to explore it on foot. I know my "exploring" day is supposed to be tomorrow, but I can't help it. Besides, I feel like the Basilica will be easier to see first thing in the morning when most of the tourists aren't awake yet. I settle my bill and head out of the square, bobbing and weaving around the plethora of people milling about.

I pick a direction and start walking. No destination, and no idea which direction I'm going. I pass over some smaller canals with couples in gondolas cuddling in close, their gondolier singing a romantic tune as he purposefully looks anywhere but at the public display of affection right in front of him. My purposeless wandering takes me to multiple dead ends, but eventually, I make it to another spot on the Grand Canal. I take in the view of the massive canal that looks much more important from the water's edge. There is a huge stone bridge we passed under this morning not too far off. I now know that *that* is where I'm headed.

Before long, I'm climbing the shallow steps with a swarm of others, passing little shops that are literally *on* the bridge. I stop in a few, thumbing through potential souvenirs for Alice. I don't find anything for her, but I think *Mom would love this* or *this is so Dad* a few too many times. I head to the railing and watch boats for a few minutes until the grief passes. I have to leave the bridge entirely when I see an elderly couple, easily in their 80s or 90s, exchange a peck on the lips. I head back down the stairs on what I think is the side I came from, but nothing looks familiar when I reach the foot of the bridge.

Fuck it. I keep walking. These paths are too beautiful to ignore. I tuck into alleys, over canals, through random town squares. Hours later, when my feet start to hurt, I have no idea where I am. I recognize none of the places of interest listed on the signs around me. I try to find the bridge again, but I am so turned around that I end up at a completely different part of the Grand Canal. The stone church that faces the water looks vaguely familiar from the Vaporetto ride, but I can't tell if it was before or after the stone bridge. There are stairs that lead directly into the water. I peek down them, but the impulsive thought that enters my mind is squashed quickly by the reality of how gross this water might actually be.

A Vaporetto approaches the nearby dock where a handful of people are waiting, so I sprint over to ask if it is going toward San Marco.

A young woman whips her straight, dark hair around, looking at me with wide eyes. "Oh, thank God, another American. Yeah, this is headed that way." She scoots closer to me, lowering her voice. "Is your significant other sick at the hotel, too?"

I give a sympathetic chuckle. "No. I'm solo the whole trip." A lump forms in my throat, realizing I'm the perfect kidnapping victim right now. "I mean, at least until I meet up with my sister tomorrow." *Good save, pretend someone is expecting you.* "What kind of sick?"

The woman rolls her eyes. "Hangover, I think. Puke *all* over the bathroom. They claimed it was the seafood we had last night, but I'm not buying it."

The Vaporetto docks and we shuffle on. I wind up in a seat right next to the woman. "Did you have the seafood?"

"Nope, and after how the bathroom smelled this morning, I think I'm not going to have any for the rest of the trip."

My gag reflex perks up at the idea, but I manage to keep a straight face. "Do you mind telling me where you ate, just so I don't end up like your partner?" I have to raise my voice to be heard over the engine.

"Some run-down place by the train station. Honestly, we were just starving when we got here, so we went to the first place we saw." She turns her body toward me, holding out her hand. "Cindy, by the way."

I sit a little straighter, shaking her hand. "Lisa."

"Well, Lisa, since we are both solo for dinner tonight, what do you say to grabbing something together?"

It's amazing how all it takes to form a friendship abroad is being from the same country or speaking the same native language. "Absolutely! I'd love to hear about your trip so far."

"Great! My partner and I have reservations somewhere, but they're in no place to appreciate a fancy dinner."

"Well, we shouldn't let the reservation go to waste."

We approach another stop and Cindy stands up. "This is my stop. Here. Put your number in and I'll text you the details."

I hurriedly type in my number, checking for accuracy before handing it back to Cindy. She gives a quick wave before she hurries off the boat. We're not even to the next stop before I get a message with the name of the restaurant and the time of the reservation. I look at the current time. An hour and a half. Just enough time to freshen up and get into something a little less...sweaty.

When I return to the hotel, the front desk gives me my room number and key. Do I need to take the elevator? No. But do I anyway, because it's one of those fancy old ones where you have to pull the metal gate closed and someone presses the buttons for you? Absolutely.

It is slow as hell, and I have to resist the urge to stick my fingers out of the gate as the floors pass by, but we eventually arrive at the top floor. I find my room number and open the door to a *massive* room. The large windows pull me like a magnet and I am greeted with a view of the Grand Canal. It's a little loud, sure, but worth it. I turn back around to take in the king size bed, giant closets, and chandelier. A whole-ass chandelier. *In my hotel room.* Mom really went all-out for this one.

I wash my face in the bathroom sink—you know, the bathroom with marble countertops—before changing into a slightly fancier dress. For some reason I resist wearing the nicest outfit I brought with me, but this one is a close second. I put on my ankle boots, my feet giving an ache of protest.

For the first time on this trip, I put on a full face of makeup. It's been too hot for the whole nine yards, so it feels extra special to look all dolled up. I have Italian TV on in the background for noise—no idea what they're saying, but I'm pretty sure there were sports scores at some point. Lots of numbers, at least. I take a few selfies in my hotel room and send them to my sister. She shoots back a picture of herself in an oversized shirt with a stain on the shoulder—probably spit-up—and a caption of "look at us all dolled up and ready to hit the town."

I really do wish she could have come on this trip. The only thing sadder than being in some of the most romantic cities alone is grieving alone, and I'm here doing both at the same time. I slip my phone into my bag, having memorized the turns it would take to get me to the hotel the restaurant is in. It is a nice stroll, but my feet are not happy with walking in these boots again. I need to stop at a bench in a small square to put bandages where the blisters only just started to heal.

Cindy is waiting for me outside the hotel. I have exchanged less than two hundred words with this woman and agreed to meet her in a secondary location. *If those murder podcasts Alice sends me have taught me anything...* I shrug, taking out my phone to turn on location sharing for my sister again. Better safe than sorry.

The restaurant is located in a courtyard within the hotel building. Vines crawl up the walls, illuminated by warm lights at their bases and the echo of the setting sun. We get a tiny, circular table in the middle.

Cindy hands me the wine menu. "I don't drink, but you are welcome to get something. We'll go halfsies on the check?"

I set the menu on the side of the table. "I can't have wine, but halfsies sounds great…" I turn to give a sidelong glance. "As long as you're not getting lobster or something."

Her eyes go wide in horror. "Absolutely not after the events of these past twenty-four hours."

"How are they? Doing better, I hope?"

"They've had a sports drink and some saltines without incident. Sort of a damper on the romantic trip to Venice, though. Hopefully they recover before we hit the more walking-intensive parts of our trip."

"I'm not sure how much more walking-intensive you can get than the city without cars."

She chuckles and looks up from her menu. "We're hiking the Cinque Terre the day after tomorrow."

We order our meals, and the waiter is rather confused that we aren't interested in any of his suggested wine pairings. Cindy outlines their whole trip for me—three nights at hotels in three of the Cinque Terre towns with day hikes in-between, then down to Florence for a few nights, and ending in Rome. By the time it's my turn to share, the first course has already arrived—a mushroom risotto that smells like *heaven*.

I keep the part about my dead parents to myself, instead simply saying, "My mom couldn't make it." I hold myself together when I say it, too, despite feeling that lump in my throat signaling that tears are imminent. I make a mental note to listen to some of my mom's favorite music and trigger a good cry tonight to make up for brushing this emotion aside. I go through the places I've visited, giving Cindy ideas for her time in Florence and Rome with my very limited experience.

She leans forward over her second course and whispers, "No, but tell me more about this guy."

I guess Rocky slipped his way into the story. Multiple times. I blush. "Yeah, he just kept showing up. He really saved my skin after that bar crawl. And it was nice to have someone to eat with." I hold my fork up in a sort of *cheers*. "Thanks for this, by the way. It's great to have conversation in English."

"Yeah, yeah. Tell me more. Did you guys..." She raises her eyebrows a few times.

"No! No. He's a total gentleman."

"Last I checked, gentlemen can fu—" She pauses, looking around to see a family seated at a nearby table. "Gentlemen can enjoy extracurricular activities, too."

"Noted, but it's not like I'll get the chance. We're not even in the same city anymore, and soon we won't even be in the same country."

"Fine, but know this—" Cindy points her fork at me, staring at me through her brow, "—if he shows up and saves you again, then that is a sign from the universe that *something* needs to happen between you two."

I laugh, knowing the last thing I need while grieving is to be doing something *extracurricular* with a stranger in Europe. I'm not going to let Cindy know that, though. She looks too excited, and shooting this down might just break her heart. "Sure. If I see him again, I will give in to the will of the universe."

Her next forkload of beef pauses by her lips. "Either that or call the police, because it might be stalking at that point." She stuffs the food in her mouth, then adds, "Fate sounds more romantic, though."

I pour myself another glass of water, unsure of how to respond. There's no way Rocky is a stalker, right? Taking a sip, I scan over the other patrons of the restaurant, just to see if he's here watching. No. Of course he isn't. Because he's not stalking me. "Yeah, let's go with fate."

We finish our meal and split the check evenly, as promised. Neither of us make a suggestion to extend the night, so we wish each other well and promise to send updates about our trips. I am almost a hundred percent certain our communication will end when our trips do, but the sentiment is nice.

The walk back to the hotel is pleasant. The noise of the day has died down, and there are significantly fewer people roaming the streets. Tables for two are finishing their candlelit dinners along canals. String lights draped over the awnings and rails light my way back. The constant drone of motors on the canal has been replaced with echoes of conversations from the opposite bank. The reflections of the lights reach me on this side, the images slightly distorted by the ripples. I snag some gelato as I'm rounding the final few turns, my stomach full but also craving something sweet. I did make sure that the lemon flavor was an appropriate color, going by Andrea's litmus of good gelato, then opted for a pistachio flavor that was green, but not *green*-green.

After a good cry to some of my mom's favorite Bob Dylan songs, I shower off the day and most of my makeup—it's a little rough without a washcloth or makeup remover—and slip into the most luxurious sheets my skin has ever touched. I bet princesses sleep in beds like this.

Chapter 8

I sleep like a log, but my body keeps trying to wake up early like I had the previous few mornings. I even go to close the blackout curtains to try to muffle the sound of the city as the more put-together tourists start their days. Not wanting them all to beat me to the palace, I eventually throw on some comfortable clothes and sneakers. My eyeliner didn't quite come all the way off last night, so I put on some light makeup to match.

The line appears before I even enter the square. It's almost double what it was yesterday. I wait a few minutes to see how fast it is moving, and it does not look promising. Disappointed, I head over to the Basilica instead, where the line is much shorter and seems to move at a good pace. The facade is enough to keep me entertained in line—so much to look at from mosaics to statues. Even the arches are decorated. When I enter, I am gobsmacked. The extravagance outside is nothing compared to inside.

I am pretty sure I accidentally say "Holy shit" out loud instead of thinking it. There is no empty space in this entire, massive building. Mosaics *everywhere*. Arches. Domes. Statues. Light pouring in from high windows and reflecting off what I'm pretty sure is real gold. The sight is beyond words, and the quiet throughout the space makes me think my fellow visitors are speechless, too.

I explore everywhere I am allowed to go—including the stairs to the balcony level of both the inside and outside of the building. A little voice in the back of my head suggests I peek into some "do not enter" areas, but that level of impulsivity would be a little much, even for my mom. Besides, if I was arrested, I wouldn't get to see what happens on that one bridge at noon.

I leave the church around eleven, making sure I have plenty of time. Walking past the line for the palace, I debate whether or not to skip the bridge and just wait. If that is how the rulers decorated the Basilica, I can only imagine what their living quarters looked like. I decide against it, though. This is the only plan with a set time and I feel like I need to be there. Maybe I'll check out the palace later today, or on a future trip to Venice if that day ever comes.

The walk to the bridge only takes me half an hour, so I wander around the area, grabbing a snack to munch on while I wait. I also snag a postcard from a souvenir shop for Alice. Small, easy to carry, and won't break in my luggage on the way home. People are waiting for gondolas at a designated spot. It's mostly couples holding hands, but there is a group of college students who look like they'll all be piling in and splitting the cost. When it's their turn to load up, I am convinced the boat is going to capsize, but it stays afloat, albeit slightly more askew than I would be comfortable with if I were in it.

Finally, it's five minutes before noon. I make my way to the middle of the bridge, but nobody else is stopping except to snap a quick picture of the canal before moving on. The sun is beating down on me and, despite wearing short sleeves, I can feel the heat baking my shoulders. I look down the canal. Is it some kind of performance? Some solar illusion? I look at my watch. 11:59. Whatever it is apparently doesn't have a lot of fanfare.

A bell tower rings out the new hour and I look around, thinking maybe it is happening on the other side of the bridge. As I turn, I am met with a face that has become all too familiar this trip.

Rocky holds out empty hands. "I would have brought flowers, but I'm not sure your hotel room would have a vase. Or a table to put them on."

So much runs through my head. My brain flashes between *Am I in danger?* and *Wow, he looks good* with a spattering of *How did I not see this coming?*

The only words I manage to spit out are, "So, what happens at noon?"

He laughs, his smile melting my small hint of discomfort. "It was just so I would know where to find you when I got here. It's a famous landmark but not super busy, which is important on a day the cruise ships are in." His eyes narrow as he studies my face. "Was it too much? Should I have just told you that my next stop happened to be Venice, too?"

My head cocks back and forth as my face scrunches. "Mayyybe. When I told this story to someone last night the word 'stalking' did come up."

He pulls out and unlocks his phone. "I swear I bought these tickets weeks ago. I can pull up the email…"

I rest my fingers on his hand and push it down. "No, it's fine. But I'm not telling you where I'm going next, so if I see you there I'll *definitely* have questions."

Rocky moves next to me, resting on the railing of the bridge. "So you tell people about me, huh?"

I rest right alongside him, jabbing him with my shoulder. "You happen to be a major and recurring character in the story of this trip."

He leans in closer, breath tickling my neck. "And how do you describe this character in your narrative?"

I shoot a sidelong glance. "Dirty blonde hair, a nice smile."

"A *nice* smile? Not charming? Captivating?" He shoots an exaggerated grin.

My eyes roll into my head. "Fine. Next time I tell the story, you'll have a charming smile. Happy?"

"Very. Now tell me, did you get a chance to go to the Doge's Palace?"

"No, the line is *insane*. I hope you already bought tickets if you're planning on going."

"Did you want to go?"

"Yeah, after seeing the Basilica I feel like it would be ostentatious as fuck, but again—the line is ridiculous."

He holds out his hand beside mine, flexing his fingers a few times. "I have a plan." I take it and he leads me back the way I came, taking a slightly different route through smaller alleys and over new bridges. The buildings feel brighter along this path for some reason. The colors are more vibrant, the sounds of the city more musical.

Before long we're back at the piazza, but instead of joining the line, Rocky leads me to a door next to the entrance. "Wait here a second." He takes out his notebook and pops inside the glass door to what looks like an administrative office. I can't hear anything he's saying, but within a few sentences, the man behind the desk is standing and shaking his hand with a smile. They talk some more, Rocky writing down some notes, laughing every so often. Rocky closes his notebook and points inside, receiving a nod from the staff member. Then he gestures to me and the man gives an even more enthusiastic nod.

Rocky props open the door and gestures for me to come in. "He's going to let us in through here."

It seems too good to be true. Skipping an hour-long wait in exchange for some light conversation? Knowing Italian apparently really helps. I squeeze by him into the office. "I see you, Pietro."

He leans down and whispers, "Only Carlotta gets to call me that. If you want to mock me, go with Robert."

"Okay, *Robert*, what did you say to get him to let us in?"

The man opens the door with a wide grin. "He told me you are on a date."

As we enter the museum through a side entrance, I turn to Rocky for confirmation. "That can't be it. Over half the tourists here are on a date."

He places his finger over his lips. "Shhh. We're in a museum."

I bring myself closer to him so I can be heard in a whisper. "No, seriously. How did you get him to let us in?"

He locks his eyes on mine as a knowing smile creeps onto his lips. "Just let me have this one secret a bit longer, eh?"

As much as I want to hound him, something in his green eyes tells me to just trust him. "Fine."

He bites his lip in joy, then leans in to kiss my cheek. "Shall we?" He stands up straight, holding out his elbow.

I loop my arm around his. "We shall."

Rocky leads me through a few rooms, pointing out certain artists or subjects of the works. He must be finding plaques somewhere I am missing as I have my neck craned to take it all in. He takes me through a council room of some sort—I'm only half-listening as he explains it, as I am so focused on the incredible detail of these paintings. Even the gold molding is captivating as it swirls and crashes over the art.

We enter an armory, where Rocky tells me to pick a sword.

"What? Are you going to tell one of the guards a joke and he will open the case for you to play with one?"

"No." He starts to laugh, but then he seems to consider it for a moment. "That'd be awesome, but no. My grandma used to come with us on trips, and whenever we were in a museum, she would have us pick out the things we'd want to take home with us. She called it 'shopping' and it was one of the best parts of the trip." He leans in closer to a display case, examining one of the swords. "It was extra fun when the museum numbered their pieces in a display case because then we would choose a number upon entering and be forced to get whatever that number is in every case." He nudges me. "You better choose a sword or else I might swoop in and take the one you want."

I purse my lips, considering my options, before something catches my eye from across the room. "Does it have to be a sword? Or can I choose any weapon?"

He shrugs. "I was going to go weapon by weapon, but if you *want* to cut straight to the crossbows, I guess we can."

"How did you know...?"

"Because crossbows are awesome." He grins.

I hadn't even realized that I thought crossbows were so cool until I entered this room, but this man gets it. I still pick out a sword to humor him, a narrower blade that would probably be easier for me to lift than the clunkier old versions. When it comes to the crossbows, though, I pick the biggest of the bunch.

"You say the swords are too heavy, but you think you can manage this thing?"

"Hey, you don't have to swing one of these around. Just point and shoot." I mock holding it in my hands. "Besides, it gives a very Buffy vibe."

Rocky shakes his head. "Just when I thought you couldn't be any more attractive, you present me with the mental image of you slaying vampires with a crossbow."

The next set of doors takes us to another council room, this one even more grand. The chairs along the wall offer visitors a space to sit and take it all in, but I want to get up close in an attempt to see each brush stroke. The paintings are like wallpaper, covering every inch with the history of Venice, as well as a giant work that takes up an entire wall depicting what looks to be heaven. The sheer scale of it leaves me in awe.

"Wow," Rocky whispers from beside me.

"Yeah, it's amazing, isn't it?" I turn to discuss with him, but it seems like he had already been looking in my direction. I shake off the realization that the 'wow' might have been for me. "This kind of stuff just doesn't exist back home."

I spend almost an hour getting as close as I can to the art in this room. At one point, I have to sit in the chairs provided and just take it all in. Rocky sits beside me and holds my hand, interlacing his fingers with mine. I squeeze, trying to acknowledge him without turning my attention from the room.

After I've studied every frame, Rocky leads me to a bridge—the Bridge of Sighs. We wait in a short line to get a glimpse out of the window of the canal below. I hear someone with an audio guide telling their partner that this was the last view prisoners got of Venice before being confined to their cells, and they would sigh as they left their last sliver of the outside world. I, too, gave a sigh as I realized the stark contrast between the magnificence of the room we were just in and the cold, stone cells complete with metal bars.

We navigate down long halls with dark cells on each side. Before long, my vision starts to get a little blurry. Rocky catches me as I wobble a bit.

"Are you good?" He pulls out a water bottle from his backpack. "Need something to drink?"

I lean against the cool wall and take a sip. "I think I'm just getting a little…" I squeeze an imaginary box between my hands.

"Claustrophobic?"

I nod as I take another sip. "Do you think we're almost through this part?"

He peeks around a corner. "Yeah, not much further from here. The next part is a little dark, too, but it has more space. We can get through it quickly, though, if you're needing some fresh air." He holds out his arm for me to take again, but this time I can feel him using his muscle to support me as I right myself.

"Don't go committing any crimes, though, or you might end up back here."

I roll my eyes at the joke, but that only throws off my balance again. Thankfully, Rocky is there to keep me stable. Black spots dance in front of my eyes for a moment, but we eventually make it through the last section where there are bits and pieces of earlier decoration of the palace that have been refurbished, and then finally out of the museum altogether.

The fresh air is, well, a breath of fresh air. My head starts to clear almost immediately, and I'm feeling back to normal after about five minutes of sitting alongside a canal.

"I am so sorry. I didn't even realize I would have issues with any of that—I never have before." I fan my face, just now realizing I had broken out into a cold sweat.

"It is absolutely fine. When I was a kid, I had a full-blown panic attack in the underground war rooms in London. Something about there being no windows and being underground just set it off with no warning." He shakes his head, eyes wide with the memory. "I couldn't imagine how much it must have sucked for all the people who basically lived down there."

I scrunch my face. "Could we not talk about small, enclosed places for a bit?"

Rocky perks up. "How about wide-open places with fantastic views?" He stands, holding out his hand for me to take.

This time, I help myself up, giving his lonely hand a consolation high-five once I dust off my shorts. "What did you have in mind? I already saw the bell tower yesterday."

He gives a little shiver. "Nope, nothing that high, but no more clues because it's a surprise. But you might want to stop by a restroom beforehand, they don't have one where we're going."

What the hell kind of place doesn't have a bathroom? "Do you happen to know where one might be?"

He points out an obvious sign right over my shoulder and hands me a euro. "It might be a pay-to-pee one."

I pop the coin into my pocket. "Appreciate it. I'll meet you back here?"

"Yes, right here. I'll need to make a quick stop somewhere first, so give me twenty?"

"Knowing women's restrooms, I might be in line longer than that."

He sets off at a jog up the block, going Lord knows where. I head into the restroom which does, in fact, have a coin-operated turnstile. Once I am inside, though, I am met with a nearly immaculate lavatory. It in no way smells like the public restrooms back home, and there happens to be an open stall right as I enter. The door reaches all the way to the ground *and* all the way to the ceiling. No awkwardly checking out the shoes of the person next to me, either, because there are *four real walls* on this thing. I might actually start to feel a little closed in again if I wasn't so darn impressed.

I end up waiting for Rocky for about ten minutes, but he returns right as the twenty-minute mark hits. "If you would kindly..." He holds out his hand for me to take, and this time I do, lacing my fingers in his. It felt nice at the palace, but even nicer now that I can focus on just us. He leads me to a dock where a gondola is waiting and I freeze.

"But you said gondolas were tourist traps!"

He bats away the idea. "I just said that so you wouldn't go before I got here. They're actually terribly fun and absolutely worth it, especially if your date pre-paid." The gondolier helps Rocky into the boat, then reaches out to do the same for me. His hands are rough and calloused, but strong as he holds my arm up in case I lose my footing. Rocky gestures to him. "This is Francesco. He is built like a renaissance statue and I absolutely understand if you end up with him by the end of the night. I mean, if you don't I might."

I give the gondolier a second look and Rocky is absolutely right—the man is a beautiful specimen. "Pleasure to meet you, Francesco."

He responds in only a nod before he gestures to the little bench at the foot of his station. Rocky and I take a seat and Rocky immediately starts to dig for something in his bag. "You know, only some gondoliers will let you drink on their boats, and even then most only let you have a single bottle of prosecco..." He pulls out two plastic wine flutes, handing them to me. "But Francesco here gave permission for these." He pulls out two canned cocktails. "Not a drop of wine in either of them. Would you rather have the raspberry or the orange vodka soda?"

"You remembered I'm allergic to wine?"

"It's a weird thing to be allergic to, especially in Italy. It is sort of a hard fact to forget." He alternates holding each can out to me.

"Raspberry. Thanks."

He splits the can between the two flutes, handing me one. "To not being alone in Venice."

I take it, holding it in the air. "To meeting someone really cool halfway across the world."

We clink glasses. Well, "clink" wouldn't be the right word. We knock them together and get a very unsatisfying thump of plastic on plastic.

The refreshing drink is perfect in the late afternoon warmth. I haven't had much water today, so at least this is somewhat hydrating, right?

We float down a tiny canal first. Buildings seem to shoot straight up from the water on each side. The waterway is so narrow that, while we can pass by one gondola just fine, I wonder if it would be able to handle three across. Before long, though, we enter the Grand Canal and I am honestly a little terrified. Vaporettos shoot past us, barely giving us time to move out of their way. Obviously it is a well-rehearsed ritual for the drivers of both boats, but to me, it is a bit too close for comfort. At one point, a local on his motorboat zooms by, and I jump away from the edge and press into Rocky. He responds by moving his drink into his other hand and putting his now-free arm around me. I take the opportunity to cuddle in a little closer. I mean, it is a romantic boat ride, I might as well play the part.

We go under the Academy Bridge and the large stone one I explored yesterday—the Rialto Bridge—before making our way back down some smaller canals. Rocky's arm is warm on my shoulders, which was a little uncomfortable in the sun, but now that the buildings cast near-constant shade, it is quite pleasant. Butterflies flop around in my stomach, reminding me of that innocent excitement I'd felt when a cute boy held my hand in the fourth grade. We sit in silence, taking in this unique experience. For some reason, I keep licking my lips. *Just fucking turn and kiss him.*

I don't. Instead, I fiddle around in the bag for the other can so I can refill my glass. It turns out there are three more, so I stop holding back on my sips. Conservation is not the goal—enjoyment is. The more I relax, the more amazing this place becomes. There is truly nowhere like it in the world. Actually, who knows? Maybe there is, but I wouldn't know having not been anywhere worth visiting before.

We are three drinks in and some of the landmarks start to look familiar. We are getting close to Piazza San Marco, and neither of us has made a move. It *feels* like someone should have made a move. "Is it over?"

Rocky looks at his watch. "These things are usually an hour, so it seems so. Did you want to do another lap?"

I reach for the last beverage in the bag. "Well we *do* still have another can."

"Say less." He turns around and speaks to Francesco in Italian.

I pour us our final drinks and scoot in close, my face pressed to his chest, his hand stroking my arm. It's been so long since I've had this kind of physical touch. The last thing that came close was the incident at the bar crawl. Before that, most of the embraces came from fellow grievers at funerals. Before that? Well, let's just say it's been a while since I've dated.

Before I know it, I am voicing my thoughts. "I want—" I cut myself off before my words can get me in trouble. What if he's just being nice? What if saying something will make this whole gondola ride *very* uncomfortable? My silence lingers a little too long.

"What do you want?" Rocky shifts so he can see my face.

I turn to look at him, his green eyes piercing, his hair wind-blown. *Holy shit, this man is really doing something for me right now.* I huff a breath. *Fuck it.* "I want to kiss you." I went with the more tame version, as I was bouncing around between saying I want to kiss him and saying I want to rip his clothes off.

His eyes immediately shift to my lips. "Good."

And just like that, we are displaying some *very* public affection. If I didn't have alcohol in my system, the little voice in my head worrying about what Francesco would think might overtake the moment, but I am just buzzed enough to ignore it.

Rocky's hands explore cautiously, caressing down my arms and legs. Part of me wants him to be more aggressive, but it feels so good to have someone who just wants to touch me with no hint of an expectation of more. The noise around us drowns out and at one point, when I come back to reality for air, I see we've been rowed into a tiny canal with nobody else around. Francesco is sitting on the back of the boat, facing away from us, watching something on his phone.

I dig my fingers into Rocky's hair, taking advantage of the privacy. His hands react by clawing my back, pulling me in closer. Time loses meaning until Francesco coughs behind us, letting us know our time is up as he begins steering us back to a dock.

Rocky takes a deep breath, his next words coming out airy. "How about some dinner?"

I comb my hair with my fingers, getting out the knots that formed during the make-out session. "Yeah. Dinner sounds good." I take out my phone to check the time. "Wait. You don't have some aunt-figure in Venice, do you? I'm not sure if I could eat that much food in one sitting again, especially after a big dinner last night."

Rocky bites his lip. "To be completely honest, I did get us reservations somewhere. I wasn't trying to make any assumptions, but I wanted to be prepared in case the surprise went well." He reaches over and fixes an out-of-place chunk of my hair. "And I am taking it that the surprise went well, but I am happy to cancel those reservations and go get a pizza and drinks if that is more your speed tonight."

"Oh my God, pizza sounds *fantastic.*"

When we get to the dock, Rocky hands a wad of euros over to Francesco, who thanks him before giving me a wink. A rush of heat spreads over my cheeks now that I realize Rocky and I had just done a very public equivalent of sucking face in the back of a taxi.

Rocky falls in next to me and takes my hand. "How about we just walk until we spot pizza that calls to us?"

"What? You don't know the three best pizza places off the top of your head?"

"No, but I do know the bar we frequented on our weekend trips, and that is in this direction." He points down a path and raises his brow.

I tuck my lips, biting back an embarrassed smile. "Just promise me that if I get drunk you'll provide door-to-door service. I don't think a rideshare is the answer this time."

He crosses his finger over his heart. "I will personally escort you to your hotel regardless of your level of intoxication, but I don't think you're going to be as drunk as you were after the bar crawl."

I give an exaggerated nod that transitions into a large step in the direction Rocky indicated. Before long, we have a stomach full of the most amazing pizza I've ever had in my entire life and are settling down in a booth in an Irish-style pub. I question the choice, but Rocky reminds me that the "can't drink wine" thing rules out a lot of traditional Italian drinks served at Italian bars.

"So you've obviously been to Italy a few times, but where else have you been?" I ask, sipping my second mixed drink.

His eyes go wide. "Where *haven't* I been? My family is really big into travel. Like, in an obsessive way."

My brow can't help but furrow. "Obsessive how?"

"Well, let's just say I lucked out being Robert Junior. My parents picked my siblings' names specifically so their initials would spell out European airport codes. Fawn has the code for Frankfurt: FRA, Grace is Genoa: GOA, and my little brother Patrick is Pamplona: PNA."

"Well, what are your initials, then?"

"RBA, and before you look it up on your phone, yes. It is an airport code. But not in Europe, so it doesn't count."

"Where is it, then?"

"Rabat, Morocco."

"So, like, super close to Europe?"

"But still not Europe, so not part of the theme. Also, it was not intended when my father was named, so it double-doesn't count."

I swirl the last bit of drink in my glass. "Something something double negative."

Rocky grabs us more drinks and we keep talking about our families, as well as his childhood travels. It isn't hard to tell that this guy grew up with some wealth, but he doesn't make it a *thing*. And he definitely doesn't make my lack of travel into a thing, either. He is just genuinely excited that I get to experience all these new things he grew up loving.

In the conversation, I make sure to avoid talking about my upcoming plans. I feel like there's about a two percent chance this guy is a stalker. Maybe three. He understands my hesitation, but something in his eye tells me he knows something I don't.

It's almost midnight before we leave for my hotel, him keeping up his end of the promise. My voice is a little louder than it should be at this hour, but at least I'm not stumbling along the canals. Rocky is right beside me, hand in mine. He is a little better at keeping a dampener on his volume, but when I crack up about how horrible his gondola puns are, he joins in.

At the hotel's front door, I realize I don't want this evening to end. I want to say goodnight, to spare any humiliation if he refuses an invitation upstairs, but I will never see this man again... At least, I'm 97% sure I will never see this man again. "The mini bar here is fully stocked...if you want to come up for a nightcap."

His smile is warm, as usual, but I can see a hint of a fire in his eyes. "I'd love to."

There is no elevator operator on duty, so Rocky takes it upon himself to close the gate and ask me, "Which floor, miss?" with an old-timey radio announcer voice. I keep glancing over at him, only to find that he is already looking at me. I bite my lips together, trying to stifle a giddy smile.

We get to the room and it is immediately clear there will be no nightcap. The door is barely even closed before I'm trying to take this man's shirt off. *Oh man, is he sexy.* It's not a six-pack or massive biceps drawing me in—in fact, he is likely on the fast-track to a dad bod based on how we've been eating—but it's the way he carries himself, the confidence in his own body that makes me want him even more. In one swift motion, he slides off my top and his hands return to warm the skin on my back. We fall onto the giant bed, kicking off our shoes on our way down.

It feels *so good* to feel connected to someone. To have his body follow your every move like it needs to be in a rhythm with yours. His lips explore the skin of my shoulder, my collarbones, my arms. I have just enough alcohol in my system to not immediately shrink away when he makes it to my belly.

I am about to apologize for how my body looks, for the extra weight I've gained in my year of mourning, when he whispers, "Holy shit, you're beautiful."

I pull his face up to mine to kiss his lips again. When I'm out of breath, I pull away long enough to get out a sentence. "Just want to be sure we're on the same page—how far are we wanting this to go?"

Rocky bites his lip. "I would love to have sex with you tonight."

"I..." My breath stutters as I realize something. "I'm not sure I'm ready for that right now." I can feel my body yelling at my mind.

"Oh." Rocky leans back, resting his head on his hand, propped up by his elbow. "Are you okay with what we've been doing so far? Do you need me to give you some space?"

I mirror his stance so we are face-to-face. "No, no. I like this. I like—" I gesture up and down his body, "—this. This is nice. I'm just not sure about sex after just meeting you this week." I wince. "I'm sorry. I feel like a tease."

He rubs his hand over my arm. "I promise you I had no expectations coming up here tonight. I can leave now if you want me to, or we can go back to what we were doing. I'd be happy either way."

"Would it be weird to ask you to stay the night? It feels nice to be close to someone, you know?"

He leans in and kisses me again, soft and slow. "I know exactly what you mean."

After part two of our intense make-out session, we fall asleep still half-dressed in our day clothes. I wake up a few times at night, part shocked and part relieved that he is still there. His light snores are louder when my head is resting on his chest, but his heartbeat lulls me back to sleep before I can consider moving.

Fingertips trace circles on my shoulder as light pours in the window.

"Good morning," I croak.

"Good morning." Rocky sounds like he's been up for a while already. "Do you think this hotel has room service?"

I rub my eyes. "You had an entire pizza last night, plus the rest of mine. How are you hungry?"

"That was almost ten hours ago. I have plenty of room for breakfast."

Ten hours? I look at my watch. Right, pizza was *before* drinks, which was well before we got back to the hotel. I still have three hours until the train, and I need to give myself an hour to get to the station. "I could swing breakfast."

I call room service, listing all the food that sounds good right now, knowing Rocky will devour anything I don't eat. I turn back to the bed, where Rocky is still lying half-covered by the sheets. He looks like he could be nude at this angle. I know his pants are still on, but the image gets me going all the same. He is smiling at me, and again his face looks so familiar. I might have met him recently, but he doesn't feel like a stranger at all.

I will never see this man again. If I ever want to do something with him, it has to be now. Right now.

Staring him down, I remove my shorts and straddle him in the bed.

What happens next is between me and Rocky.

Well, between me, Rocky, and the poor room service guy who rolled the tray in while we were dressed in bedsheets and out of breath.

Chapter 9

Rocky rides the Vaporetto with me to the train station and navigates my suitcase through the crowd. He seems to instinctively know how the flow of people is about to move, and helps me make it to the platform right as the train arrives. He hands over my bag and pulls me in for a kiss. His face lingers near mine, goodbyes unable to escape our lips, until the voice over the loudspeaker lets us know that it is time. I kiss his cheek once more and turn to go. He grabs my hand, pulling me back in for one more kiss. He squeezes my hand and lets go, leaving me with a piece of paper in my palm.

I rush to the door, stow my bag, and find my seat, the paper digging into my hand all the while. Once I'm settled, I open it, recognizing the paper from the notepad next to the phone in the hotel—its name sprawled across the top. Underneath is a hand-written phone number.

Part of me wants to keep this perfect, to not contact him ever again and remember this as the most wonderful fling I could possibly imagine. I use my phone to take a picture of the number but don't put it in my contacts. This way I can keep my options open on whether or not to contact him, even if I lose the note. I tuck it into my *Bob Adams* book, taking out my mom's itinerary when I realize I didn't even look at her plan for yesterday.

> Day 6:
> Check out the Doge's Palace/Basilica
> Bask in Venetian excess
> Let Lisa do something special for herself

I nearly spit out the sip of water I have in my mouth. *Yeah, more like some*one *special*. I scold myself for having the sense of humor of a twelve-year-old boy, then look to the next day.

> Day 7:
> Train to Verona
> (if time, Juliet's Balcony?)
> Train to Munich
> U-Bahn to hotel
> Pretzels and Beer!

The ride to Verona is quick, and the train to Munich doesn't arrive for a little over an hour. I look up how long it would take to get to the balcony. About half an hour. I can walk there, take a peek just to say I saw it, and walk back with time to spare. Perfect.

I change my mind as I exit and see this looks nothing like a city center, and it is probably not super walkable. I snag a taxi right outside and am whisked away along the river to the heart of Verona. The taxi leaves me a short walk away, but it is easy to see where to go—just follow the swarm of people coming into and going out of an archway.

There is no rhyme or reason for getting in or out, so I have to take a deep breath and force myself and my bag into the crowded entry. The stone walls on either side are dark with layers upon layers of messages for the fictional dead girl. It makes the space feel even smaller. My bag catches on the uneven stone floor. I turn around to pull it free but bump into someone. Before I can even turn around and apologize, they are pushing me right back, trying to get out. I finally make it to the courtyard and can breathe a little easier, but there are still bodies *everywhere*. All cell phones are cast upwards, toward a small balcony on the second story of the house on our right. It's a nice balcony, I guess, as far as balconies go, but they know it's not actually her house, right?

I take my phone out and dutifully take a photo. It's not like I will be showing my mom anytime soon, but she would want the picture. I see a steady stream of people making their way to a statue in the corner of the courtyard, and initially join it, until I see that almost every single person who hoists themselves up to pose places their hand on her breast. In fact, the statue's breasts shine like they were just polished, while the rest of her is the bronze of a statue left on its own. Her arm shines, too, where people hold on so they don't fall off the platform.

A mother pushes past me with her teenage daughter in tow. "Come on, it's good luck!"

The teenager pulls back, freeing her arm. "Mom, I don't want a picture of that."

"Fine. At least take my picture while I do it? My love life needs all the luck it can get." She hands her phone to her child.

The daughter rolls her eyes. "Ew, Mom."

Luck, huh? I suppose I could use some luck. But it's still weird, groping the statue of a girl. How old was Juliet, anyway? A teenager, right? Besides, it's not like she consented to having a bunch of tourists all up on an image of her. I shake my head. *Juliet is a fictional character.*

The main question I should be asking myself is why my mom would have wanted to come here. She must have had more reasoning than just, "It's something to fill the time while we wait for the next train."

I look back at the mom, her hand firmly grasping Juliet's breast. Did my mom want luck in finding someone new? *Of course not. She still refused to throw out Dad's old clothes and still wore her wedding ring.* It was for me. She wanted a son- or daughter-in-law and decided that throwing coins in fountains and touching a hormonal teenager's bronze breast would at least help me get there.

I sigh, tucking myself into the line. It isn't too long before I am beside her, hoisting myself up onto her platform while keeping my other foot on my bag so it doesn't disappear. I whisper, "Sorry about this," before lightly grazing the back of my knuckle along her sideboob and hopping back down. Even if she isn't real, even if it was probably why my mom wanted to come here, it still felt weird. I roll my eyes at myself. *No more peer pressure from a dead woman, please.*

It takes a few minutes to navigate back out of the courtyard and onto the street. Part of me wants to go back and read some of the notes, but most of me just wants to be out of that crowd. I peek at my watch. I have a few minutes to spare, so I head back down the street to the square I saw on my way in.

There are stalls set up in the middle of the square selling all sorts of souvenirs and snacks. I grab a cup of fruit and a pastry before making my way back to the street to order a rideshare. As much as I would have enjoyed exploring the market, I don't want to miss my train.

I arrive with time to spare, which is good because apparently in Italian, Munich is called Monaco. I had to check my ticket a few times to make sure I wasn't going on a very different trip.

Once I board, I cram my bag into the luggage rack above me, plop down in my seat, and pop in my earbuds. After that courtyard and my rideshare driver talking my ear off for the entire drive, I think I am done "peopling" for a while. A gentleman sits down in the seat facing mine across a tiny table and immediately buries his face in a newspaper—I'm glad we're on the same page.

It's the first time I'm awake and alert enough to notice the scenery as it zooms by, and I am not disappointed. We glide between lush hillsides that are soon dwarfed by massive mountains behind them. I am so entranced that I don't even notice that my playlist ended. I only notice the silence when a snack cart comes rolling through the aisle and the man in the seat across from me waves his hand to let me know. I get a sandwich and a beer, then I'm back to being hypnotized by the landscape of, what I believe at this point, Austria. I'm unsure if it's the altitude, the beer, or even just the beauty outside my window, but something about this train ride puts me completely at ease. I get to sit in one place while actually zooming at over a hundred miles per hour through the Alps, gliding past fucking *castles* perched on top of hillsides. We make it high enough to see snow and ice in the dead of summer.

The guy across from me is also mesmerized, his newspaper still open, resting on the table. He says nothing until we pull into Munich, and even then he only gives a grunt and acknowledging nod as he folds up his reading material.

After a long day of travel, I am too tired to figure out logistics on my own, so I ask the tourist information desk for instructions on getting to my hotel. It's a pretty simple subway ride and a short walk after. The stroll is pleasant, thanks to the break in the oppressive heat I'd been experiencing so far this trip, as well as the serious lack of cars in the city center.

The hotel is nowhere near as glitzy as the one in Venice, going back to the budget trip I had expected, but the room is still pleasantly cozy. I drop off my bags and plop down on the bed. It's amazing how exhausting sitting for six hours can make you. I close my eyes for what I expect to be maybe five minutes, but when they open again I am disoriented. I look at my watch. It's seven in the evening—I was asleep for two hours.

I sit up in bed, but my head protests. I just want to stay here and rest. My stomach weighs in with its need for sustenance. The hotel doesn't have room service, so I do need to figure that out. I rummage through my bag. I have my emergency energy bar, but that just doesn't sound appetizing at all.

It takes me almost half an hour to muster the energy and walk to a little corner shop. I stand in the snack aisle, dead eyes, staring at the labels that are a mix of German and English. I could go for the safe snacks, the brands I'm familiar with, but something about those currywurst-flavored potato chips calls to me. I snag what I assume are some cheese puffs, but for some reason, there are peanuts on the outside. I guess I'll figure that one out when I'm back in the hotel room. A trip down the candy aisle adds some gummies and chocolate-topped cookies to my armload. I'm barely balancing everything by the time I get to the cashier.

Once I'm back in my quaint little room, I open every bag and sit at the foot of the bed, watching the episodes of Downton Abbey I have downloaded on my phone. I wish I could be sitting here bingeing German snacks and British dramas with my mom. I finish the one where her favorite character dies and, knowing Mom would have needed some time to recover from that episode, I end there for the night.

Chapter 10

When I wake up the next morning, I am surrounded by half-eaten bags of junk food. Surveying my feast, none of it looks appetizing, but it certainly hit the spot last night. I pick up my phone, wanting to text my mom something about how traumatic they made that death scene, but alas, someone else probably has my mom's phone number by now. Holding my phone in my fingertips, I open my photos. The most recent one is of a castle in the Alps, but just before is the phone number. *I could text him...* No. Venice was perfect. Let's keep it that way.

Bob Adams' Adventures is sitting on the bedside table, Mom's notes tucked inside. I didn't get around to pretzels, but that can be squeezed in today. What else is on the itinerary?

Day 8:
Viktualienmarkt
Nymphenburg Palace
Bratwurst, Schnitzel, and Spaetzle

I blink a few times trying to figure out what the hell the first word is or how to say it. I gather that the second one is a palace and the third is easy enough to figure out—I will clearly not go hungry in Bavaria.

After showering off the remnants of the currywurst chip smell, I get dressed and head downstairs for the hotel's breakfast. I expected more sausage but am greeted by the same familiar continental breakfast I've had nearly every morning. Jelly on a pastry, some cheese, and a bit of fruit later, I'm off to explore.

The woman at the front desk points me to the Viktu–Viktuali– to the market. It's not too long of a walk, and I get to stroll through the main square, Marienplatz, right by a beautiful gothic building. Part of me hopes this is the palace I'm going to hit up later, but it seems more business-y than homey.

The market is fabulous. I fall in line with some strollers and elderly folks with their rolling shopping bags. There is fresh fruit, but not pre-cut and packed in plastic to-go containers like some of the other markets. Most of the offerings are ready for someone to take home and put into a meal. There are cute cafes with some ready-made food, as well as fresh-baked pastries and pretzels, but the market itself seems to be mostly catered to the people who live and work in this city.

The flower stalls call to me and I take out my phone to capture the vibrant colors on display. A young vendor shouts something at me in German. It sounds angry.

Wide-eyed, I shrug, then say, "English?" My heart races.

He smiles, then points to a sign. I half-expect it to say "No Pictures" or something, but then I notice it has a social media handle on it. With the same cadence to his voice, and at the same volume, he says, "If you post, please tag!" He no longer sounds angry, though. Something about the German language just sounds so…intense.

There weren't too many visitors when I got here, but it seems like a flood of people suddenly decided it was time to go to the market. It becomes more and more difficult to go to the stalls I want as the flow of people pushes me along. My face gets hot and my clothes feel like they're shrinking, pushing in on my chest and constricting my lungs. I try to slow my pace, but people are bumping into me on all sides. My eyes dart around for an opening. They lock on a mom, who looks at me with concern, then hurries over, pushing her kid's stroller.

"Bist du okay?" she asks. That phrase doesn't sound angry, and the worry in her tone is clear.

I press my eyes shut and shake my head. My whole body is hot now, and as much as I'd love to de-layer, I don't have any layers to lose.

The woman grabs my hand and places it on the handle of the stroller. "Halte?"

I open my eyes to see her holding onto the handle, gripping it tightly and shaking it to emphasize what I am to do.

I nod, grab on, and the stroller takes off, pulling me along. The woman is yelling loudly, and the river of people parts—either they are locals who understand her or the tourists are just startled by someone yelling. We make it to what looks like a grove of trees where the crowd is not quite gone, but at least better organized. People are sitting at long tables in the shade, drinking.

My guide takes me through the entrance and leads me to a table on the edge of the cluster. After parking her stroller behind me, she grabs her child and leaves. The quiet and shade are already helping me calm down, but for good measure, I fan myself with my hands. "What the fuck was that?" I ask myself.

"Bat duh buck," a voice babbles from the stroller.

I lean over to see there is a second seating component in the stroller with a toddler inside. Did this woman seriously just leave one of her kids with me and bounce? I wave at the little blonde boy. "Hi."

He waves back, beaming a smile, then returns to twirling a toy octopus around his arm.

I look around. Where the hell did his mother go? I'm not even sure if I got a good enough look at her to be able to pick her out of this crowd. A new panic sets in, but at least this time I'm not focused on myself. I stand up to see if I can spot her, but before I can move I hear a noise on the table behind me.

With one arm, the mom is holding her infant, and with the other, she is setting down two mugs of beer. She scoots one in front of me, then mimes drinking. When I take a sip, she nods with a smile.

I'm pretty sure that suddenly being in charge of another human being was what got me out of my head, but the beer is helping to settle my nerves just a bit more. It also brings down my body temperature. I can feel the flush slowly leave my face and chest.

The mom fiddles with stuff under the stroller and pulls out an applesauce pouch for the toddler and a bottle for the baby. She comes back around the table for a sip of her beer before asking, "Brezel?" while gesturing to the table next to us, where a couple is sharing a pretzel.

This is weird, right? A stranger is giving me beer and buying me food, without even speaking the same language. Or maybe it's just a mom looking out for someone who had a weird freak-out in the middle of a market. I nod. My mom wanted me to have a pretzel, and now this mom is offering me one.

"Halte?" I recognize the word from before, but now she is handing over her baby. I'm a little startled at first, but my arms move to take it. She hands over the bottle next, and suddenly I am feeding this woman's baby and making sure nobody walks off with the stroller with the toddler in it while she, I assume, goes off to get pretzels. Either that or she is off to go live the child-free life of her dreams.

Thankfully, she returns after a few short minutes, trading me a pretzel for her baby, who is already finished with the bottle. The toddler is still "eating" his pouch, but I'm pretty sure he just blew it up with air and is pretending to eat it at this point. The pretzel is warm, fluffy, absolutely perfect with the cheese dip she brought. It's a delightful complement to the beer, which is now half-gone.

My new mom friend, whose name I still don't know, places her coaster over her beer whenever she scoots away to care for the kids. At first I assume it is a "don't get drugged by a stranger" type of thing, but when leaves and debris fall from the trees above us, I realize it is much more innocent than I thought.

We continue to drink together, not saying much, only one or two odd words to try to ask something. It is using this method that I find out the dip is called obatzda and the beer is brewed in Munich.

I pull out my *Bob Adams' Adventures* and open to the section on Munich. It is a pretty short chapter, and I bet the specific *Bob Adams Germany* book would have had more, but I wasn't going to bring each country's book on this trip. Besides, my mom planned the whole trip with *this* book. The Viktualienmarkt was right there at the top of the list of things to do, followed by the Marienplatz, English Garden, and Nymphenburg Palace. I guess my mom just chose some of the top-rated sights for our one full day in the city.

The baby starts to get fussy, and even after some burps they still seem upset, so the mother starts packing up her things. I try to slide her a ten euro note to pay her back for my snack, but she just stares at it before continuing to put her stuff away, leaving it right on the table. She grabs both mugs in one hand and pushes the stroller with the other, giving a wave and what I assume is a goodbye in German before leaving me alone.

I pull up a map on my phone and see that the palace is a ways away. It also says that public transit would only take a few minutes longer than getting a rideshare, and is significantly less expensive, so I opt for the subway and get there in about an hour.

As I approach, huge fountains splash, their droplets scattering sunlight across the surface of the massive ponds. I take a trail that sets my gaze in the dead center of the palace, overlooking the largest pond. It is the most peace I've found on this trip outside of a church. Despite the throngs of tourists heading into the building, this area is quiet and still. I almost wish I could just stand here for the rest of the day, but Mom had plans and I want to stick to them.

The palace itself is beautiful. You can tell that they had plenty of space to play with, unlike the Doge's Palace which was limited by the size of the island beneath it. The use of gold is more dainty, too. While the Venetian palace seemed to use gold as a building material, this one uses it as decoration, accenting the molding instead of dominating it. The huge windows allow the sun to bounce off the lightly-colored walls and make the spaces seem bigger.

Once again, my neck is sore from gazing up at the paintings on the ceilings. There is so much art as I travel from room to room. I try to read some of the placards set up, but after a while, I just want to move on to the next room, especially in the smaller spaces where people seem to bottleneck.

I'm a little on edge, to be honest, and I start to worry about having another one of those episodes. The worry makes me even more uneasy, and my heart starts to race. I quicken my pace, hoping to get outside into the fresh air sooner. Part of me wishes I had someone with me right now. My mom could snap me out of this, I know it. Even Rocky, who could somehow tell me exactly how much farther I would need to go before we got outside. Maybe. No. He's the Italy expert. He wouldn't know about Germany. But he would probably know of some game to distract myself right now.

Still, I take out my phone and open the picture of his phone number. My phone asks if I would like to save the number. I say yes, then start a message. I have to look at a sign near me to get the spelling of the place right, though.

Lisa: Is there any, like, quest I could do at the Nymphenburg Palace? There are no weapons, so that one is out.

I look around the large room for a bit. It is scarcely decorated, so most of the tourists just pass through, giving me more space to myself.

Rocky: Lisa?
Lisa: Yeah. Sorry.
Rocky: I haven't been to that one, but you could always try to find the least comfortable chair.
Rocky: Don't sit in them, though. They don't like it when you do that. Just by how they look.
Rocky: Munich, huh?
Lisa: Yeah. Leaving tomorrow, though.
Rocky: Have you been to the main square yet?
Lisa: Passed through it.
Rocky: You should go back and really check it out. If you make it by five the clock does a little show. Not that great, but it's what the tourists do.

I look at the time. I could probably be back by then. I put my phone away and hurry through the rest of the rooms, stopping to take a picture of a chair whose designer clearly had aesthetics in mind rather than comfort.

When I leave, I take a walk through the park behind the palace. It's a little bare, mostly just grass and paths, and feels almost like I am walking the track at my old high school—complete with geese hanging out in the field.

I take the subway back the way I came, and I can hear the clock chiming as I enter the square just after five o'clock. A crowd is gathered in front as little figures play out a scene for the onlookers. When the music and figures stop, the crowd gives a little applause, but then the scene below starts with spinning dancers. When that ends, there is a pause before the applause, everyone obviously unsure if this was the actual end or if a third act was coming.

"Not something to write home about, but now you can say you've seen it."

I keep my eyes on the clock tower, knowing I imagined the voice.

"I probably could have told you I was going to be here, but I like surprising you more."

I turn to my right and Rocky is standing there, also staring up at the now-still figures. My stomach drops. "I *just* told you I was here. There is no way you could have taken the train all the way up here in that time." I shake my head and take a few steps away. "How did you know I was going to be here? Did you..." My eyes shoot open with realization. "Did you memorize my itinerary when you looked through my stuff at the bar?"

The smile on his face drops. "Lisa, I swear." He pulls out his phone. "Let me show you one thing before you jump to any conclusions."

I cross my arms, but stay where I am. "Fine. One thing."

He taps a few buttons and shows me an email. It's a confirmation for a train ticket in his name for today, from Verona to Munich. "So? Obviously you got here somehow."

"Look at the date it was sent." His voice is a strange mixture of amusement and pleading.

I look. Three weeks ago. Before we even met. "How the hell do we have the same plan?"

He gives me a knowing smile. "I have a theory, but we will have to test it out for your next city, which you will not tell me. If we end up in the same place, then I'll be almost certain I'm right."

The coincidence is unreal, but the date confirmation tempers my nerves. "But if you're wrong, then this is the last time we will ever see each other?"

"I think it went pretty well the last time it was the last time we would ever see each other."

I can't help but let a smile creep onto my face remembering that night...and that morning. "Do you think you can top a romantic evening in Venice?"

"It depends, what did you have planned for your last night in Munich?"

"Honestly, I just want to find somewhere quiet. Somewhere away from people and noise. I feel like a sardine in a can."

Rocky bites his lips together, holding back a ridiculous smile. "Oh, this is perfect." He grabs my hand and pulls me toward the large gothic building and through a door into the tourist information office. When we get to the counter, he asks for someone by name.

"What is going on?" I ask as we wait off to the side.

"Just trust me."

An incredibly tall man comes out from a back room and shakes Rocky's hand.

"Guten Tag, I called earlier." Rocky swings his backpack off his back and pulls out an envelope. "This is from my boss."

The employee opens the letter and reads through it. "Yes, thirty minutes, then I must close." He leads us outside and through a large, open door into a courtyard surrounded by this gothic building, towering up on all sides. It really is a gorgeous structure. We head into one of the doors, through some corridors and finally, he stops at a door, pointing to it but not opening it. "Thirty minutes."

My brow furrows. Wait. Munich doesn't have legal brothels, does it? I peep my head around Rocky as he opens the large, creaking door.

Let me tell you. It is— it's just— holy shit. I enter the room and am met by a library straight out of a fantasy novel. Large wooden tables line up along a wall of nearly floor-to-ceiling windows. Flower-shaped light fixtures seem to grow from the wall in swirling stems and leaves. The other walls are three stories of dark wood bookshelves with spiral staircases and railings covered in creeping metal ivy.

I pick my jaw up off the floor and look at Rocky. "What is this place?" My voice echoes in the empty room.

"It's a law library," he whispers and swings his backpack onto a table, taking out a really nice camera. "My boss wanted some pictures, so I had to come after it closed for the day." He snaps on a new lens and fiddles with some buttons before snapping a picture of me. "Is this quiet enough for you?"

"Yeah, I think so. Can I...?" I point to a bookshelf and he nods, so I scurry over to read some of the titles. Of course, they're all in German, and the ones on this level are behind glass cabinets that I'm afraid to open. I hear Rocky's camera clicking away behind me and turn to see him getting close-ups of the staircase and windows. "Do you think the pictures will take half an hour?"

"No." He grabs his bag and hands it to me. "In fact, I think I can be done once I get a few of the whole room. If you stand behind me, I can get it completely empty."

I go back to the door and he backs into me, apologizing before taking his shots. "I thought you were an editor, not a photographer."

He pulls the camera from his face and starts to look through his pictures. I peek over his shoulder to see how he captured the warmth of the room and the amazing details in each element. "I mostly edit, but I also do some research and other odd jobs while I'm on these work trips." He comes across a picture of me looking at the books. "What do you think?"

I scoot in closer. "I look kind of pretty in that one."

"That's because you *are* pretty. I don't think I could get a bad shot of you." He takes his bag back. "Here. Go up the staircase."

I hesitate, not sure if we're allowed to explore.

"Go! We have the whole room for—" he looks at his watch, "—twenty-four more minutes."

I walk across the room to the amazing spiral staircase, grazing the polished wood with my fingertips. There is nothing roping it off, so I start up, curving to the left with every step. I can hear Rocky's camera at work, but now I'm curious what is up here.

The second floor has more books, but these ones are not behind a protective cabinet, so I pull one out and flip through the pages. It looks dense. *Of course it's dense. They're law books.* I shake my head and place it back on the shelf.

"Come to the railing," Rocky calls up in a yell of a whisper.

I oblige, resting my hands on the rail and posing with a smile.

Rocky shakes his head. "Nah, that's not going to work. I want to see the smile you gave me yesterday morning."

"What smi—?" My eyes get wide as I remember what happened yesterday morning. "Oh. I'm sorry, you're going to have to work harder to get me there again." I walk down the second-story balcony, dancing my fingers across the top of the railing playfully.

He snaps a few pictures of me, but I can see his smile from behind the camera. "I feel it should be easier this time around."

"Ah, yes. But even though we do have a history now, I am also not fully convinced that you are not stalking me."

He takes the camera from his eye, his face pleading. "I showed you the train ticket!"

"Yet you already claim to know my next move. Maybe you'd been stalking me longer than I'd known of your existence." Of course I'm toying with him, but the paranoid person in me sends up a red flag because this last statement could actually be true.

"If I see you in your next city, I will tell you how I know, and it will explain everything."

"Then why not tell me now and let me trust you a little bit more?"

"Because I want a repeat of Venice."

I lean on the railing, stretching my arms out, giving him my best coy grin. "My place or yours?" I'm mostly joking, but being alone with him is bringing up that want again.

He looks at his watch. "We have this room for twenty minutes..." He pulls his camera to his face immediately.

My mind races with images of him having his way with me on the wooden tables, pinning me against the bookshelves, or having his head between my legs while we're hiding on the staircase. I bite back my grin and stare at him.

He clicks the camera a few more times and then checks the images. "There it is."

"Are you serious?" I ask.

He laughs. "No. I'd lose my job for sure if we were found out. But I did get that smile." He turns the camera around to show me, but I'm too far away to see.

I rush down the stairs, leaping off the final two in order to see this picture. There I am, with a dreamy smile on my face. I'm pretty sure he captured the moment I was thinking of the staircase. "That's the smile?"

"That's the smile." He pulls me close and places his lips by my ear, whispering under his breath. "And I would be honored if you would let me see that smile again tonight." He pulls away, then returns to his normal whisper. "But for now, we read." He throws his bag on the table once more, putting his camera away and taking out a book with golden swirls on it. He pulls out a chair and sits, pulling out a seat for me, as well.

I take out my *Bob Adams* and plop it on the table.

Rocky reaches over, grabs it, and shoves it back in my bag. "This is about *escaping* the chaos of the real world." He opens his bag and pulls out another book, this one with a woman on the cover with her hand on fire. "My sister lent me this one. It's not the *best* book I've ever read, but it's not bad. I like the world-building."

The book has been read multiple times, as evidenced by the cracked spine and dog-eared pages. Maybe the whole family had read it. I sit down next to Rocky and dive into a world of vampires and demons and monsters. At one point I am pulled from the story by Rocky's hand on mine, but once we lace fingers I am able to get right back into it.

Twenty minutes later, Rocky's watch starts to beep and we pack up. I try to hand him the book.

"No, keep it. Something to read on your train ride tomorrow."

I squeeze it into my own bag, and we head for the door just as the man who brought us here walks in. "Did you get your pictures?"

"Yes. Thank you so much."

He turns off the lights and locks the door behind us, then leads us back to the front of the town hall, where Rocky and I stop, looking out onto the square.

Rocky sighs. "Man, now I really wish we would have. Firing be damned. I could probably get another job."

I jab him with my elbow. "Probably be more comfortable in a bed or on a couch." I pull out my phone and open my photos from the palace. "Just not in this chair."

He recoils from the image. "Yeah, nope. Not that chair. Those solid wood tables would be more comfortable than that."

I start to walk forward, but not before leaving Rocky with, "I was thinking the staircase."

He doesn't follow immediately, but waits a few beats before hurrying alongside me. "Now I really regret it."

I roll my eyes. "How about dinner? I am told I need to have..." I pull out my mom's itinerary for the day. "These things." I show him the paper, but don't let go when he grabs it.

"Bavarian classics. I think I know of a place."

I pull the paper back from him. "Of course you do. What? You dated someone from Munich and came up here often?"

"No. There are just some places I intended to visit and one of them is a classic Bavarian restaurant. This is actually my first time here."

"Oh. Alright then, lead the way."

After some wandering trying to find the place without using a map, Rocky finally caves and looks it up on his phone. We apparently walked by it twice already. When we're seated, we go over the menu, but I barely skim it.

Rocky looks up from his menu. "You're really trying to stick to that list, huh?"

"It's what my mom wanted to do. I feel like I should honor it." I shrug. "Besides, I like having a set plan of what to do. It's not a perfect itinerary, but it's at least a guide for my day."

"Down to what you're going to eat? I mean, you know both bratwurst and wienerschnitzel are traditionally made with veal here, right?"

"How do you know I don't eat veal?" I ask.

He looks back down at his options. "You went with the chicken in Italy because you weren't sure you wanted to try veal."

"You remember that?"

"I try to remember everything I can about you, Lisa."

I smile, then look at my menu. Of course, it's in German. "Do you think they have menus in English?"

"Want me to order? I can get you something traditional that doesn't have veal. Oh, and the spaetzle. That *is* something you're going to want. Flipping delicious."

"Sure." I set the menu back down. "Wait. Do you know German?"

He laughs. "No, but I know German *food*. Is pork okay?"

"Yeah, pork sounds great."

The server comes and takes the order, Rocky bouncing between English and perfectly-pronounced German food names with a "Danke" at the end.

He turns to me. "I know it's what your mom wanted to do, but if you stick to the itinerary, you might burn out before the end of the trip. Did she plan for any down days? Time to recover?"

"I don't know. I only look at the plan the day-of," I admit.

"If she was here, you two would probably be making changes and modifications to the plans. Jumping from sight to sight is going to take a toll on you pretty soon."

I have an urge to tell him about my freak-outs today, but decide against it. "I'll be fine. I can recover when I get home."

Rocky gives me a disbelieving look, but whatever he is about to say is interrupted by the beers set on the table between us. He holds his mug up and says, "Prost."

I assume it is the German *cheers*, so I "Prost" back and we clink glasses. Rocky takes what I think is a big sip, but when I start to lower my glass, his eyes issue a challenge. He is chugging his beer. I tilt my mug back up, narrowing my gaze. I went to house parties back in the day—I could do this upside-down if I needed to. I let gravity help me out and open my throat, chugging about half the beer before my stomach realizes what is happening and protests. I stop for a breath, Rocky staring at me while still taking slow pulls, and I let out the most massive belch I have ever created in my entire life. A demon might as well have left my body and it would have been a less startling experience. I cover my mouth and squeal.

Rocky does a spit-take, his eyes wide. He grabs his napkin to wipe the beer from his chin while laughing. Other tables are staring, either from my table-shaking burp or Rocky's hysterical laughter. I want to hide my face, but the menus are gone and all I have left is my beer, so I bend down to whisper to Rocky behind it. My worry shifts from myself to him when I see his face is beet red and it looks like he can't breathe.

"Are you good?" I ask.

He coughs a few times, manages a few deep breaths, then finally leans in close to respond. "Are *you* good?"

"Just a little embarrassed. I think the whole restaurant heard that." I look him up and down. "And my date thought it was a little too funny."

Rocky shakes his head. "No, no. I was just shocked that *that* could come out of you. I'm pretty sure burping is fine here. Also, I am impressed both by the burp *and*—" He slides his beer next to mine, "—the fact you drank more than me." My beer is a good half-inch lower than his.

I sit up a little straighter and look around, noticing that everyone else has gone back to their own meals and conversations, before giving a hair flip. "Just one of my many talents."

"And what are your other talents?"

I shoot him a knowing smile and a wink. "You'll just have to find out."

Rocky bites his lip and shakes his head.

The food comes—a giant hunk of pork on the bone, some dumplings, sauerkraut (I recognize this one), and a noodle-y thing covered in cheese. Rocky gestures to it all, indicating that we can share everything. It's no surprise I go for the cheesy carbs first, immediately realizing that this is a food I need to have in my life. Buttery, cheesy, absolutely delicious. The pork falls off the bone, the dumplings are starchy and delicious, and the sauerkraut...well, I never liked sauerkraut and today is no different. The meal wasn't refined or fancy, but could definitely be described as *satisfying*. Good, hearty food.

Together, we finish off every plate. The waiter asks if we want anything else, but I am pretty sure that, between the two beers I drank and the heavy food, I am about to burst. Or maybe I just really need to burp again. Either way, Rocky pays for the meal and we head off.

Rocky tucks his hands into his pockets and shrugs. "English Garden?"

"I feel like we're a little far away from England..."

"No, it's a huge park in Munich I wanted to visit while I was here. It'll be light out for a bit longer—want to walk around with me?"

While I was sort of hoping to take him back to my hotel and jump his bones, maybe letting myself digest a little before activities would be a wise move. "Yeah, sure."

We venture a little way from the restaurant and pass through an archway in a long wall, which takes us to a path lined with trees on one side and old-fashioned street lamps on the other. Not four steps into our promenade, the lanterns flicker on, as if the groundskeepers had been waiting for us to arrive before illuminating them for the evening. Rocky takes my hand, lacing his fingers with mine. We walk at a slow pace, allowing people in a hurry to pass us as we soak in the quiet and company. We meander on any path we can find, cobbled and paved, past ponds and streams, over bridges. We even go through a tunnel that gives us momentary privacy, where Rocky pins me against the wall and steals a long, breathless kiss. The second a family can be heard entering, though, he saves face by pulling my eyebrow up with his thumb, staring into my eye, and saying, "I don't see anything in there, maybe it's some dust or something?" I can't help but crack up, even though that kiss sent a new wave of wanting through me.

Eventually, and clearly through no planning since we were completely engrossed in conversation, we find ourselves back at the gate we arrived through. The question I ask no longer feels impulsive. It feels right. "Your place or mine?"

"I am once again in a hostel for this leg of the trip, so unless you want an audience, yours would probably be the better bet."

We are back to my hotel room in ten minutes, even though the map app said it would take fifteen. Maybe I'm a *little* eager. We don't even get through the door before his lips are on mine, his hands all over my body. He half-carries me into the room, with me walking backward on my toes toward the bed. I step on a few snack bags from last night on the way, but neither of us pay any attention to that.

Over the course of the night, he exceeds my expectations of what might have happened on that library staircase, I show him how well my ability to open my throat and stifle my gag reflex for chugging beer translates to other areas, and we discover that day-old currywurst chips make an even better after-sex treat than cigarettes.

Chapter 11

The TV is still on from last night, playing some German morning news show. I hear it as I stare up at the ceiling. Rocky's head lays on my chest and I don't want to wake him. This is the only place I want to be right now because right now it is still perfect.

The problem is, I really like Rocky. When it was a one-night fling, it was easy to leave him, but now I don't want to because it might actually hurt this time. Now that I know there is a chance I might see him again, it will break my heart if I don't. My heart. Oh shit, do I love Rocky?

I press my eyes closed. *No. You just met this guy. You're trying to form attachments because you're alone in the world.* I shimmy out from under Rocky's head, but he's still dead asleep. Sitting on the side of the bed, I turn around to look at him. God, he's cute.

I try to tidy up quietly, picking up the chip bags with a two-finger pinch to make as little noise as possible so he can keep sleeping. His backpack and my bag are right next to the door. Some things fell out of his, so I shove it all back in, including—get this—his own copy of *Bob Adams' Adventures*. I thumb through it quickly and see it is *filled* with notes, dog eared pages, and even tabs sticking out of the sides. This guy really researched.

I sneak back into bed as best I can, but he wakes up regardless. "Good morning," he says with a smile. His morning breath is awful, but I kiss him anyway. It's not like mine is much better.

"Good morning. Not to hound you first thing, but I'm going to need some answers."

His smile grows. "I'm not telling you what my next city is. You will have to wait until tomorrow to find out."

"It's not that." *Even though the suspense will be killing me for the next 24 hours.* "You gave me so much crap for having a copy of *Bob Adams* but you have one in your backpack."

His smile falls instantly and he sits up. "You went through my stuff?"

"No!" I match his posture. "I just noticed you had it and saw that it was all marked up, but I didn't go through your stuff."

He looks me up and down, his brow furrowed. "How did you get the book if you didn't go through my bag?" He throws the sheets off himself and immediately scans the floor for his clothes, gathering his boxers and putting them on.

"Some stuff fell out of your bag. I was putting it back." I stand, too, and glimpse his shirt. I have the urge to kick it under the bed without him noticing but decide against it, instead picking it up and holding it out to him.

He takes it, but instead of putting it on, he balls it in his hands for a while as he studies me. After a long silence, he finally asks, "Do you promise?"

"I promise. It was considerably less rummaging through a bag and guidebook than you did on the first night we met."

He tosses his shirt down on the bed and pushes his messy hair off of his forehead. "Fair. But that was to get you home safely, not snooping." He lightly elbows me, his smile back.

"I was not snooping! I was cleaning." I playfully shove back, and he falls onto the bed. We make out for a bit, but as I straddle him I pull away and say, "I was scared you were going to leave for a second."

He looks up at me, his eyes looking from one of mine to the other and back. "I was about to, but you've trusted me so much this past week, I thought I could return the favor."

I lean down for a kiss, then continue the conversation. "Can I ask why you were so concerned about me snooping?"

He reaches up, delicately running his fingers through my hair draped alongside our faces. "There's just something I'm not ready for you to know yet. Pretty soon, the puzzle pieces will fall into place and you'll figure it out, but I'm hoping to hold off as long as I can—to keep this perfect."

My concern over his words is canceled by the last one. He, too, wants to have this perfect fling. To make his trip even more memorable. To keep my memory as a souvenir as I plan to keep his. Maybe the dark secret he's hiding isn't so important. "Just promise me it isn't something horrible."

"It isn't something horrible." He rises up to give me a quick peck on the lips. "Now, what time is your train?"

We have enough time to freshen up, take a *really* long shower, and then get my bags packed.

He can't take me to the train station today—he apparently has some work stuff to do—but he gets me safely to the subway. I get to the station right as my train is *supposed* to leave, but it's delayed by about a half hour. Once a few other trains leave, a seat in the waiting area opens up and I relax and scroll on my phone for a while. Curious, I pop Rocky's name into a search engine to see if anything comes up. *Wait... I don't know this guy's last name.* My eyes widen. *I slept with this guy multiple times and I don't even know his last name.* Well, here's hoping my birth control works.

I sit with this revelation for a bit, trying to force myself to remember him telling me his full name, before a call comes over the loudspeaker for my train to Zurich. My luggage fights me all the way to the platform, but I make it with time to spare. I get myself situated in my seat, my bag barely squeezing overhead, and just begin to settle in before I realize... *My layover was ten minutes.* I pull up the train reservations and see, yep, unless the train goes fast enough to make up twenty minutes, I am definitely missing my next train.

I groan so loudly that the mother at the four-top next to me gives me the stink eye. I wave in apology before taking out my book. I *could* search for other trains and times, but I have no idea what the policy is for missed trains and if I can still get a refund if I rebook myself, so I plan to go to the ticket counter at the Zurich train station when I get there. Instead of getting stressed, I lose myself in a story, which is great, because it makes the three-and-a-half hours breeze by, with an occasional glance out the window at some more gorgeous scenery.

When I make it to Zurich, it seems I'm not the only person in need of a schedule change. It takes me twenty minutes just to make it through the line, and I even hear another train for Geneva call for boarding as I'm almost to the front.

The woman working has a pasted-on smile that I know, deep down, she does not feel in the least. Her eyes are telling me that she's either at the end of her shift or at the end of her wits...or both. She politely explains in accented English that I *just* missed the train to Geneva, that the next one is full, and that there is only first-class available on the train after that. She is hesitant to waive the upgrade fee since my first train was run by a different operator and it's not this line's fault that I missed the connection, but she eventually concedes and gets me onto that train, meaning I am now delayed only an hour and a half overall.

I peruse a bit, looking at my lunch options, before opting for Burger King. Is it haute Swiss cuisine? No. Is it what I really want right now? Absolutely. A Whopper and fries, Coke on the side, and my American tummy is thoroughly pleased, though I was intrigued by some fancier options I'd never seen in the States featuring different cheeses and mushrooms.

I get onto my next train and settle into my first-class digs. It's really nothing too fancy, but I'm not one to complain about comfier seats and a quieter car. I pull out my book and quickly remember that a major plot twist just happened, so the next three hours fly by as I finish the book just twenty minutes before we are due into the station—perfect timing to look over Mom's itinerary for Geneva.

Day 9:
AM Train Munich > Zurich > Geneva
Cathédrale de Saint-Pierre
Do Fondue!

My groan for *another* church is quickly silenced by the promise of melted cheese. I check the opening hours for the cathedral and it seems like I should be able to tuck in before they close. I'm not really feeling like spending hours there, anyway. I just need to swing by my hotel and drop off my bag, which will be super convenient because it is blocks from the cathedral.

One bus ride and a short walk later, I am feeling good about navigating on my own. The city is beautiful. Honestly, I hadn't even really considered it a destination to visit until my mom popped it on the itinerary. I step into the hotel, passing by the proud five stars on its plaque out front. *I guess Mom got fancy on this one, too.*

"I am sorry, ma'am. We don't have that reservation."

My heart drops. "What do you mean?"

The woman at the front desk shakes her head, her hair in a tight bun with nary a hair out of place. "We had a reservation for Diane West, but not for Elisabeth."

"I should be on Diane's reservation. That's my mom."

She taps the keys a few more times. "On her notes, she has Elizabeth with a *z*—" She looks down her nose at my ID still on the counter in front of her, "—and you are with a *s*."

My jaw drops. My own mother misspelling my name, and she was the one who freaking chose to spell it with an *s*. "So because my name was misspelled you won't let me have the room?"

She finally looks away from the computer and gives me the most stone-faced stare I have ever seen in the service industry. "No, we will not let you have the room because when we called Madame West to confirm the reservation two weeks ago, she did not return our call. Our emails, too, went unanswered. We allowed someone else to book in your place, and now we do not have a room for you. We are completely booked." She hands me back my ID and credit card.

My jaw clenches. *What the actual fuck?* I am tempted to yell at her about the fact my mom would have a hard time answering because she's *dead*, but it won't magically open a room. It *might* magically make me burst into tears, though. I give up, hoping to save myself some grief. "Where am I supposed to go?"

The woman huffs then picks up the phone and dials a number. My high school French can't keep up with her, but she glares up at me every few seconds. She finally cracks a smile right before she hangs up. "I found a spot for you in a hostel." She pulls out a map and circles a location on the other side of the city. "They will hold the bed for you as a favor to me. You're welcome." She explains how to get there, but it ends up amounting to getting back on the bus I was just on, in the opposite direction, and then walking for another fifteen minutes. I could pull out my phone and search for last-minute hotel deals, but a hostel is probably the only thing in my budget, especially for a last-minute stay. The only reason I've been able to stay in all of these places is because my mom paid for them in advance. Any inheritance I might get is in limbo with a lawyer right now. I can't afford to be fancy.

The experience at the hostel is at least more hospitable. The woman behind the counter is smiling, so that's a start. She books me into a shared dorm for the next two nights, points out where the lockers are, and reminds me that breakfast is included. She even hands me a bus pass so I can navigate the city for free. I store my bags and check my watch—not enough time to get back to the cathedral before it closes, unfortunately, but I still have plenty of time to get myself into a cheese coma. While the woman at the front desk encourages me to make some friends in the common room to go out to dinner with, I politely decline—if I have to share a room with five other people tonight, I will take my chance to rest in peace during my meal. I leave with two suggestions of restaurants that do fondue on the same street, about two blocks away.

While my earlier adventures across the city were simply to get from Point A to Point B, this is the first chance I get to truly *enjoy* Geneva. And holy shit, is it *clean*. The other cities were nice, yes, but they were like well-lived-in homes. Geneva is like the pictures of the house while it's on the market—everything is *just* so. The ground isn't littered with cigarette butts. The traffic noise is present, but not overbearing. The air smells *fresh*. Maybe this city is exactly what I need to avoid burnout.

I come across the first restaurant recommended, but don't want to cut my walk short, so I go the extra couple hundred feet to the second one. It has outdoor seating and I am able to ask for a table for one in my broken French.

I was determined to rely on those four years of high school French for these last legs of the trip—Switzerland and France—but it is all of two minutes before I pull out my phone to make sure I'm not accidentally ordering veal or something I'm not going to like. There's adventurous, then there's foolish, especially with these prices—I mean, it's charged per person, but even for one it is *not* cheap.

I go with the classic gruyere. There are loads of options, but I feel kind of guilty Googling the name of each and every one.

Besides, if I like it enough, maybe I'll come back tomorrow for something more fun.

The incredibly cute waiter with blonde hair falling over his eyes comes to ask for my order. Well, I think he does. He speaks so quickly that I have no idea what words shoot from his mouth. It seems like the right time to tell him what I want, though.

"Fondue maison, s'il vous plaît? Et une tasse d'eau," I manage to say, my face scrunching with the attempt.

He scribbles down the order with an amused smile. "Americaine?"

I let out a sigh of defeat. "Oui."

"Water with or without bubbles?"

"Sans gaz. Merci."

He disappears for a minute before coming back with a glass bottle of tap water and a glass. I sip as I people-watch. The other outdoor tables have groups of people laughing and talking over their shared bowl of hot cheese. One group is speaking English, excited for their outing to Mont Blanc the next day. One keeps trying to convince everyone else to go do an escape room they found. Personally, I'd do the escape room.

Other groups speak French. I can pick up on words here and there, but eavesdropping is not super successful when you aren't fluent in—or even half-decent at—the language.

My fondue comes and bread to go with it. I was thinking there might be some more things to dip, but honestly, carbs and cheese seems to be the motto for this trip, so I take it gladly. I am instantly confused when the waiter sits down in the empty seat opposite me.

"It is no fun to eat alone," he says as he leans deep into the chair. "Je m'appelle Gabriel."

I finally relax my brow. He's just on his break. "Lisa."

We get through some pleasantries—him speaking slowly and allowing me to use my rusty French. He's from this area, but not Geneva proper, is an only child, and wants to get a job working for the local government. He's the perfect companion as I stuff my face with cheese, some of it dripping off my chin as I take a little too ambitious of a bite. *Man is this delicious, though.*

Eventually my French vocabulary runs out and we switch to English.

"I am finished working at eleven," he drops casually as he scoots his chair back out.

Gorgeous? Check. *Ambitious?* Check. *I'll never see him again in my entire life?* Probably also check. So why am I trying so hard to come up with a reason to say no?

The only thing standing in my way is the thought that Rocky might be here tomorrow. I mean, he probably won't be...but he *might.* There has been no mention of any kind of exclusivity, and I *could* go out with Gabriel guilt-free, but I just...don't want to.

"Lisa?" Gabriel must think my brain is short-circuiting. "I must get back to work."

I shake myself from my train of thought and smile. "Eleven is pretty late for me. Thank you for the company, though."

"Is there anything else I can get for you? A glass of wine, perhaps?"

I look down at my half-finished meal. "No, thanks. I'm good. Besides, I'm allergic to wine."

His eyes go wide. "You do know that fondue has wine in it, yes?"

My smile drops. "It what?" I can now place the subtle tang I had been tasting along with the smoothness of the cheese—white wine.

Gabriel leans over me, studying my face. "Do you need me to call the doctor?"

I feel my cheeks and lips. I've never had one of those severe reactions, but the way he is looking at me makes me think I must look like a balloon. Everything is still in place, though. "No, no. It is nothing life-threatening." *I'll just have an uncomfortable morning tomorrow...*

Gabriel leaves to get me my check, and I stare at the cheese. It is so tempting to take another bite, but I am already going to be suffering enough tomorrow, no need to add salt to the wound.

As I walk back to the hostel, I just keep hoping Rocky will show up tomorrow. I take out my phone and send him a message.

> Lisa: Any chance you'll tell me where you're going tomorrow?

Not even a block later, I receive a reply.

> Rocky: Nope. But if I'm right, you need to be prepared with a bathing suit and a nice dress.
> Lisa: You forget that I already have plans, wherever I am.

Rocky: You forget that I also predict you are going to be burned out if you don't get some downtime.
Rocky: See you tomorrow.
Rocky: Hopefully.

Getting back to the hostel, I grab my bags and make my way to my room. There are three bunk beds—and the only one that looks open is the bottom bunk closest to the door. Nobody else is here yet, even though it's starting to get dark out. Maybe I'll meet my roommates later, and if not I can see them tomorrow.

I buy the eBook for the sequel to the book I finished on the train, and read it on my phone. This one is about mermaids. Not sure I'm as into it, but I'll give it a few more chapters before I give up. That will have to be later, though, because my eyes are starting to droop. I throw the covers over my head so I can sleep through anyone turning on the lights and promptly pass out.

At one point I wake to the sounds of one of my roommates having some *intimate time,* so I let out a loud cough to alert them to my presence and they put a stop to it with a whispered, "Sorry! Sorry!"

Chapter 12

My nails are digging at my skin before I am even conscious of the motion. The scratches leave more of a burning trail than a pain. I try to take a peek at my chest, but my eyes have a hard time adjusting.

"Hey, uh, new girl," I hear a female whisper from somewhere else in the room in a thick Australian accent. Or maybe New Zealand? I can't tell the difference at this point. It's still pretty dark and the shades are drawn, but I can see the outline of someone getting dressed.

When nobody else responds, I take it as my cue that I must be the new girl. "Uh, yeah?"

"Sorry about last night. I didn't think anyone was in here. Hope we didn't wake you up or anything."

I wave her off. I'm not in the right headspace to reassure her or berate her. I'm honestly not even sure which one I would do. On the one hand, I understand giving in to certain urges on a trip abroad. On the other hand, this is a *shared* room. Instead of responding, I pull the covers back over my head and turn toward the wall, pretending to go back to sleep until she sneaks out.

I pull my phone out and use the flashlight under the covers to check the damage. My chest is covered in red splotches, some of them raised with large streaks of scratches across them. Apparently I went to town on them last night without even realizing. No wonder, too. They itch like a bitch. I rummage through the toiletry bag I left under my pillow and pull out the lotion, spreading it all over my chest and neck, and tucking some into my armpits just in case. I try to get back to sleep, but I end up just nodding in and out of consciousness as my roommates each start their day one by one. Once nine hits, any semblance of trying to be quiet is thrown out the window, whose shades are now completely open, letting the bright sunlight in.

I get up and head toward the women's restroom to take a cold shower, hoping it will work in tandem with the lotion to at least stop the itching, if not make the hives disappear completely. Thankfully, there are individual stalls and not six people to a shower, so I get some privacy as I stand in the downpour of near-freezing water. If I wasn't miserable before, shivering in the shower just puts the cherry on top. This attempted cheese coma might actually kill me.

I put on some more lotion as I get myself ready for the day, but I know it is going to need something more hard-core. It looks a *little* better, but this is a pretty bad reaction. Maybe a pharmacy will have some Benadryl or something. As I rummage through my bag, I spot my bathing suit. I have no idea why I even brought it. I have not seen a body of water I would touch with a ten-foot pole yet. Maybe the creek in that park in Munich, but I'm not sure—it was so dark when we walked by and I was a little...distracted.

I remember going over a bridge (twice) yesterday, and that river connected to a body of water, but I didn't get a great look at it. Maybe I will investigate later. But even if it *did* look swimmable, I am not going swimming, because one, I am not about to show off my hive-y chest, and two, Rocky is *not* about to show up.

Once I'm ready, I grab my small bag with my *Bob Adams*, my mom's itinerary, and my wallet, and store everything else in my locker. I grab a bit of breakfast from the little buffet and head on my way. Thanks to my detour yesterday, I know exactly which bus to grab and remember seeing a pharmacy on the way to the stop. The pharmacist thankfully speaks English, but it takes a few searches between my phone and her computer to figure out what the Swiss equivalent of the American version of Benadryl would be.

When she pulls a box from behind the counter, she comes back with a skeptical look on her face. "It will make you tired."

"I know. But at least it will help with this." I undo a few buttons on my top and show her a glimpse of the hives.

"Oh, yes. It should help. Just be careful." She hits a few buttons on her register. "And go to your hotel if you begin to feel too tired. I do not want you falling asleep at a museum. The workers will be sad to think their exhibit made you so bored."

I buy a water bottle and some snacks to throw in my bag and pop my first tablet. It's not pink. It feels weird that it isn't pink. Hopefully the antihistamine kicks in soon, though. My shirt rubbing against the hives makes the itch come back something fierce.

I hop on a bus—for free this time, thanks to my bus pass—and make my way back over to the cathedral. I completely spaced that today is Sunday, so I end up having to loiter outside for half an hour while services finish up. There is no entry fee, so I get to just walk in once the masses are allowed inside. I expect to find glittering mosaics or giant frescos, but in the end it's just...stone. The architecture makes up for the lack of color, with giant gothic arches and intricate columns, but I am sort of glad I didn't have to pay admission.

I did, however, want to check out the view, which Bob Adams said was worth the extra fee, so I pay my ticket and march up the stairs. I must be getting pretty fit on this trip, as I am not nearly as out of breath as I thought I'd be by the time I get to the top. However, it is the view that takes my breath away. Swatches of old, red roofs scattered among more modern buildings, gorgeous mountains in the distance that I overhear someone say is actually France, the vista stretches in almost every direction.

But the most prominent feature is a massive plume of water shooting into the sky from the massive lake, which is surrounded by docks and beaches. *Oh my gosh. Rocky is coming to Geneva.* My heart flutters and excitement buzzes in my skin. This is ridiculous, though. I am here to do this trip for my mom, not to get all goo-goo-eyed over some guy.

I reach into my bag to pull out my mom's itinerary.

Day 10:
Some museum...
Another museum...
Eat Swiss chocolate

Paraphrased, obviously. But I'm not feeling the museums at all. Rocky might be right. I might need a day to relax (and recover from my allergic reaction). At the very least I need a nap before I tackle one of them. I can get behind the chocolate, though. That one won't take any convincing.

I get back on the bus to the hostel. At this point, the Swiss Benadryl has fully kicked in. I try to stay alert by searching for the best chocolate makers in Geneva on my phone, but I'm having a hard time keeping my eyes open, so I lean against the window and let my eyes flutter shut. A rustling at my side slowly wakes me up, but I don't comprehend what happens next in my dazed state.

All I know is that the person next to me got off the bus in a bit of a hurry, but when I look down at my bag, it is open just enough for a hand to get in and out. The bus is moving again before I can investigate and—yep—my wallet is gone. The gravity of this realization jolts me awake. *Oh, shit my wallet is gone.* My driver's license is gone. My credit card is gone. *All* of the cash I had for the trip is gone. My jaw sits slack as I dig around, convinced if I keep looking, my wallet will appear under my old itinerary papers or my water bottle. But it never materializes. It is with that woman I barely caught a glimpse of. I dig more to find my phone but feel a wave of relief when I realize it is still tucked between my thighs, right where I put it when I started to give in to sleep.

Lisa: I think I was just pickpocketed. What do I
do?

While I wait for a response, I sit there feeling violated for the rest of the ride, and even part of the walk back once I'm off. That woman had her hands all over my stuff. That woman has my credit cards. *Oh God, that woman has my credit cards.* I open my banking app and freeze one card right away, but I have to call my other bank to freeze my backup. When I hang up, I have a message waiting.

> Rocky: Are you alright? What did they take? If they got your passport, go to the police station to report the theft—that's the only way the embassy will give you a replacement. Did you cancel your cards?
>
> Lisa: Took care of the cards already. Passport is safe at the hostel. Not much of a chance of getting a replacement for my coffee punch card, though, huh?
>
> Rocky: I'm waiting for the train to Geneva now. I'll be there in a little over three hours. PLEASE tell me you're in Geneva.
>
> Lisa: I'm in Geneva.
>
> Rocky: Thank God. Where are you staying? I'll meet you once I'm in town.

It feels like a tiny part of the weight I'm carrying has been lifted off my shoulders. I send a screenshot of a map with my hostel circled.

Rocky: You aren't going to believe this...
Lisa: What?

He sends back a screenshot of his reservation for a private room in the same hostel. *You've got to be fucking kidding me.* I check it again, and the screenshotted email is dated months ago. *Clearly* not stalking. I wasn't even supposed to be staying there.

Lisa: And you're going to explain all of this when
I see you, right?
Rocky: Yes. It's time.

I get back to the hostel and lay down in my bed. I feel so dumb for just leaving my bag next to me like that. It was like I was *inviting* her to take my stuff. I pop another Benadryl so I can power nap and hopefully sleep off these hives. As I wait for it to kick in, I take out my *Bob Adams* and run my fingers over the worn cover. At least she didn't take the whole bag, I guess. I still have the itinerary and the guidebook, these last pieces of my mother. I flip through the pages and stop on one with a giant Post-It note as a bookmark: a section titled "Pickpockets in Europe." On the note, my mom's handwriting reads, "Make sure Lisa reads this."

A little late, Mom! I throw the book on the foot of my bed and bury my face in the pillow. I wake up to the sound of my phone buzzing right by my head. Groggily, I can see there are a few missed texts, but someone is actually *calling*.

"Hello?" I answer.

"Hey, are you here? I'm at the hostel, I want to be sure you're okay."

I wipe some drool from my lip. "Yeah, no. I'm fine. I'm here. Just had a lie-down and fell asleep. I'll be out in a bit."

I sort my things, checking one more time *just in case* my wallet was just misplaced. Nope. Still gone. My head is in that "may cause drowsiness" fog, but it feels like I might be on the upswing. The nap was a good idea.

Seeing Rocky right in front of me as I leave my room is a breath of fresh air. The fog in my brain clears as my heart gives a little flutter in my chest. *My chest.* I pull open the collar of my shirt and peek down. Still a little gross, but much improved from this morning.

Rocky's face contorts. "Checking to make sure they're still there?"

I freeze. I probably should have checked *before* leaving the room. "Uh...no. I woke up with some serious hives this morning."

I can see the gears turning in Rocky's head. "You had fondue, didn't you?"

I lower my head like a child caught with their hand in the cookie jar. "I had fondue..."

"Should have gone with the raclette. All the ooey, gooey cheese, none of the wine." He pauses again, looking me up and down. "Will you be alright in the sun?"

I finally take a second to get a good look at him. He's sporting board shorts and a baggy shirt. Much less put-together than he normally is. "You weren't kidding about bathing suits, huh?"

He smiles. "Not in the least. We both need a break."

"And while we are on this break you're going to explain everything? Why you're following me? How you keep getting us into places? What the hell I'm supposed do after being pickpocketed?"

His eyes narrow. "I will answer most of those."

I glare right back, unsure whether or not I want to accept this. Who am I kidding, though? I want to spend time with him regardless of this ongoing mystery. "Fine, as long as you answer the stalking question."

His brow shoots up. "Well, I would like to clear my name in regards to stalking, so go ahead and open your *Bob Adams* to page 317."

I swing my bag off my shoulder and rummage for my travel guide. Flipping through, I find the right page.

Under the title "Bob Adams' Two Week Itinerary: Rome to Paris by Train" was a list of destinations and travel days—the exact one my mom must have used to plan the trip. I stare at the page. "So we're on the exact same trip?"

"Yep. You just started one day ahead of me."

"Which means you'll be in Paris, too?"

"Arriving the day after you do."

The smile on my face is the dopiest. Paris with Rocky? It seems too good to be true.

Rocky cuts into my daydream. "But right now we are headed to the police station to file an official report about the theft. They won't get your wallet back, but having it documented will help you out in dealing with any fraudulent charges. You're sure they don't have your passport?"

"I can double-check now, but I'm pretty sure I left it in my locker."

He glares and gives a skeptical grunt.

"What?"

"Normally the advice is to bring your passport with you, but I guess in this instance leaving it here was the right choice."

"Should I bring it with me now, then?"

"For filing the police report, you'll probably need some form of ID, so yes. But we can come back and lock it up before we go to the beach."

After I snag my passport and shove it in the bottom of my bag, Rocky and I head to the police station. At one point on our walk, I feel tears welling in my eyes. I suppose I had been in such a state of shock that I hadn't processed just how violating the whole experience was. This woman's hand was in my bag without me even realizing it. She has my driver's license in her possession. If my mom were here, she would have sat in that seat next to me. She would have made sure I was staying awake on the bus. I slow to nearly a stop to gasp out a cry.

"Hey. Hey." Rocky puts his arm around me and I turn into him, bawling. "Let's find a place to sit."

He walks me to a public bench under some trees. My face is on fire, but the light breeze in the shade feels nice on the tear streaks. "I'm sorry," I sob. "This is just a lot."

"It is. It really is. But after we file this report, we will do nothing for the rest of the day. I'll get dinner, I'll lend you some cash to tide you over until Paris, and you can figure out everything with your bank there to hopefully get some money transferred."

Oh my God. Money. I start bawling all over again. "I hadn't even thought about how I'm going to pay for things."

Rocky pulls me into his chest and just sits there as I cry, rubbing my back every so often. By the end of my outburst, I feel calmer—still upset, mind you, but at least I feel like I can breathe. I sit up, using the bottom of my shirt to wipe my nose.

"You ready?" Rocky asks.

"Yeah."

We finish the walk to the police station and it is a quick process for them to take my story and I get assigned a case number. The process is almost seamless, and the officer couldn't look more bored, so I assume they do this pretty frequently. On my way out, I get a, "Be more careful with your things." I give a pressed-lip smile in response, then roll my eyes as I leave the doors. *Obviously.*

On the walk back to the hostel, I pull out my mom's itinerary. "What do you think I should do today?"

Rocky takes the paper and looks at the three bullet points. "I think you should go to the lake with me." He hands the list back. "We can buy some chocolate on our way."

I look at my mom's handwriting. "My mom really wanted to see these museums, though. Not going would be rejecting this plan she made for the two of us."

He turns around to face me, stopping us in the middle of the sidewalk. "Exactly. She made the plan for *both* of you. She's not here to enjoy it with you, or even to explain *why* she wanted to share these things with you. If she were going to make a plan for you on your own, I am sure it would look different. If she saw the shit you're going through on this trip, I'm sure she would call an audible and do something fun for the both of you. That's what I'm trying to do now. I'm trying to find a way for *us* to have fun together because according to my itinerary, *we* only have a few days left." His gaze bounces between my right and left eye, almost pleading.

It does make sense, though. My mom wouldn't want me to struggle through. She would want me to enjoy this trip. And be spontaneous. Plus I do want to spend more time with Rocky. I look back at my mom's paper. This is the last day of her version of the itinerary. There's one more sheet behind this one, but I have the official plans for Paris. I thought my eyes were all cried out, but one more tear makes its way down my face as I give a silent apology to my mother before stuffing the itinerary back into my bag. "Should I go get my swimsuit?"

Back at the hostel, Rocky offers to put my passport in his room. He has a private room with a real safe, so that would be two layers of security versus my locker in a very public space. I agree, but only if I get to be the one to put it in and set the code. The feeling he was stalking me still lingers in the back of my mind, even though it has been all but disproven, so I thought it would be best if my passport was not entirely in his control. He even leaves his room key with the front desk and gives them permission to give it to me if I come back without him. This also makes it so we can bring only the essentials with us—his ID and credit card in the pocket of his swim trunks and a few hostel towels to lie on.

We stop by a grocery store on the way and pick up some sodas, bread, cheese, deli meat, and some fruit for a picnic lunch-dinner combo, as well as a bit of sunscreen. We also stop into one of the local chocolatiers and *oh. My. Gosh. The smell.* I could have been standing next to a vat of melted chocolate and had a similar sensation. The rich aroma of cocoa permeates the entire room. I try to refrain from asking for everything in the store, especially since Rocky is the one paying, but we end up with a small bag of things to try as well as a promise we could stop again on the way back when we weren't going to be sitting in the sun.

When we make it to the beach, I can see we weren't the only ones with this idea. There are throngs of people on the beach, as well as plenty of folks squeezing onto a little dock for a little extra sunshine reflecting off the lake. It's not a *beach* beach, though. The images of Caribbean blue waves crashing on golden sand were quickly replaced by reality. The shore is all pebbles, and honestly, I am here for it. I hate sand. It gets everywhere. Not to mention the texture is so grating. Instead, I take off my sandals to feel smooth stones under my feet. They hold the sun's warmth and it soaks into my body through my soles.

A family down near the water is packing up to leave, so we scurry over to take their prime real estate once they go. Their kids are a little red from the sun, so I immediately lather up with sunblock. Not about to add peeling to my current skin woes. I take off my shirt and see that the hives have almost completely subsided. At this point, nobody will think I have some sort of contagious rash.

We have our picnic in the late afternoon sun, the laughter of kids and the splashing of water as our background music.

"So, if you're here for work, why are you going off a *Bob Adams* itinerary?"

He looks at me for a bit, as if he isn't sure if he wants to answer, but then gives in. "That's actually who I edit for. I'm helping update the guidebooks and part of that is to follow an itinerary to make sure it's still doable."

I take a moment to finish the massive bite of sandwich in my mouth. "No way. That has to be one of the coolest jobs ever. Do you know Bob-o?"

He lets out a little chuckle. "Yeah, he's...a great boss."

"Is that how you got us into the palace? You name dropped?"

He nods, his eyes a little wary.

"And that's why you have so many notes in your guidebook. And the notepad you carry around, too." I take a sip of my drink. "It explains so much." For some reason, Rocky almost looks to be in pain, so I change topics. "Is the water safe to swim in? It looks sort of...green." I gesture to the slime that is coating the rocks closer to the water.

Rocky nods to the crowd of people in the lake itself. "They seem to be alright. Besides, if we need to clean up when we get back, I have a private shower in my room."

I shimmy my shoulders. "Ooh, private shower. How fancy." It's mostly a joke, but I will definitely take him up on that offer instead of using the public ones again. I stand up and brush the crumbs off my legs. I'm still not one hundred percent on going into a lake with algae, but if I don't go now, I will probably never be able to psych myself into it. "Shall we?"

Rocky's eyes go wide while he watches me take off my shorts, fumbling to take his own shirt off. "We shall."

As I walk to the water, I stop to glance back at our stuff. It's literally just two towels, some clothes, and a mostly empty grocery bag. It's fine. Nobody is going to take them. Letting out a sigh, I turn back to the water to see Rocky running until he is hip-deep then doing a gentle dive in. My feet slip a bit on the rocks, but it seems the green stuff is not as concentrated on the water's surface as it is on the shore.

"Water's great!" Rocky encourages as he brushes his hair with his hands, flicking some of the water off into the air. The droplets catch the sunlight in the same way as the giant spray of water from the massive fountain in the lake.

I dip my toe in, expecting something horribly glacial. While it is a contrast to the heat of the air, it feels refreshing. I am able to wade in comfortably until it hits the sensitive skin of my belly, at which point I cringe and my face contorts, but I keep my forward momentum.

Rocky comes to greet me, his mouth under water but his eyes watching me. When he makes it over, he pops up, points his face toward the sky, and spits a stream of water into the air. After it comes crashing back down onto his face, he looks at me and says, "Guess what I am?"

"Someone who is going to get sick from some random lake bacteria?" I guess.

He points over his shoulder with his thumb at the fountain. "No. I'm The Jet."

I roll my eyes. "You are a child."

"Well, it looks like the children are having much more fun than the grown-ups, so I think I will join them." His hands thrust forward, sending a wave toward me.

I barely turn my head in time to not get a mouthful of water. When I turn back, I shake my head. "Don't you dare."

His eyes narrow. "Oh, I dare." He splashes me again.

I lunge after him, but he ducks under the water. I spend the next few minutes chasing him, half-running and half-swimming in the shallow water. When I finally catch him, I'm pretty sure it's because he took pity on me and slowed down. He wraps his arms around me, and his wet skin against mine gives me chills. "What, were you on the swim team or something?"

Rocky laughs. "Crew, actually, in high school. But thanks to some clumsy guys that kept getting put in my boat, we did a bit of swimming." He doesn't take his eyes off of me, biting his lip as he pulls me even closer. He kisses me and it feels good enough that I don't even worry about whatever lake bacteria might still be lingering on his lips.

After some more horsing around, the chill sets in and we head back to shore to dry off in the sun. Surprise, surprise, our towels and clothes are still there. As is the bag, although the two chocolates we saved for later are no longer holding their shape. "Still have your cards?" I ask, worried they might have fallen out during our activities.

Rocky pulls the ID and credit card out of his pocket, shows me, then tucks them back in. "We're good."

I sit back down on my towel and take out the chocolates, resorting to ripping the bag open and licking the confection off the sides because eating it with my hands was not going to be a tidy experience. I offer some to Rocky and he takes a few licks as well. For a while, we sit in silence, watching the Swiss enjoy their summer evening, before lying down to soak in some rays. Rocky's hand finds mine and they join over the warmth of the rocks between our towels. When it is time for me to rotate to my stomach, his hand finds the side of my thigh instead, rubbing it with the back of his hand. Everything feels perfect, just as it should be, right in this moment.

The only thing that would make this better would be a book—probably the one I bought on my phone. It seemed like it would be a nice beachside read.

As most of the other beachgoers start to pack up, Rocky and I join them, donning our clothing and heading back toward the city.

"You know what sounds *amazing* right now?" Rocky asks.

"A long shower in a private bathroom?" I suggest.

"Yeah, that, but also a quesadilla."

"You really think we're going to be able to get a quesadilla in Switzerland?"

His phone is already out. He holds up his search results. "Surprisingly, yeah." The first result is right by our current location, and the first review picture is even a quesadilla.

"Let's do it. I'd love to see how the Swiss do Mexican."

Rocky holds out his elbow and I link arms with him. For a few seconds, we skip along together, until our feet get out of step and it becomes an awkward bob. We settle for holding hands as we walk, our towels slung over our shoulders.

While the restaurant offers burritos and tacos, a quesadilla just sounds perfect, so I get one with chorizo. Rocky goes for plain cheese. I promise to pay him back, but he insists that today is his treat. Man, was Rocky onto something, because the food absolutely hits the spot, to the point I almost forgot we were going to swing by the chocolate shop again on our way back to the hostel. This time we go for the alcohol-filled varieties.

Rocky invites me to move my stuff into his room and I am happy to accept. As I roll my bag past the front desk and towards Rocky's door, the person who checked me in gives me a knowing wink. I can't even deny it, though, because once I'm moved in, we hit the shower together and do things I wouldn't dare do in a public shower.

Once we're out and in our pajamas, we sit on the bed, eating boozy chocolate. Rocky helps me call my bank and get a wire transfer of some funds to a bank in Paris so I can pick it up when I get in tomorrow. We talk about life and traveling and about our childhoods until the wee hours of the morning.

Chapter 13

Thank goodness I set an alarm last night because my body would have *loved* more sleep. The good news is I have a long train ride ahead of me. The bad news is I'm not sure I can trust myself with falling asleep on public transport again.

I let Rocky stay sleeping as long as I can, attempting to get ready in silence, but once I'm about to head out, I climb on top of him and plant my lips on his.

"I'm headed to the train station. Thought I'd say goodbye."

He tries to sit up but finds himself pinned and falls back onto the pillow. "Let me walk you there."

"It's really okay," I say.

"I insist."

"Fine. But get dressed quick. I don't want to be late."

"Deal." It takes him two minutes. The longest step is when he smells a shirt a few times to make sure it is still good to wear. "Let's go."

He holds my hand the entire way, leaning over to kiss my head any time we are stuck at a crosswalk. It feels so nice. It feels so natural. I can admit that I am starting to feel something significant for Rocky. I shouldn't, because this fling has one city left, then we will be out of each other's lives for good. But I will let myself feel this feeling—for now.

I stop just beside the entry, turning to face him. "I think I got it from here."

"Oh, wait. I actually needed your help with something. You have a second?"

I look at my watch. Twenty minutes until departure, but the station isn't too complicated. "You have five minutes. What's up?"

Rocky walks me over to the wall to get out of the way of the other travelers coming and going. "Did you go into the cathedral?"

"Yeah."

"Did you go...*up*? Into the towers?"

"Yeah. Lots of stairs, but it was pretty manageable."

He nods a few times, his brow furrowing. "I am supposed to write about what it's like up there, but I...uh...am not sure I'm going to have enough time. Do you think you could shoot me a text with the highlights?"

"Oh my God. Were you skipping work to hang out with me yesterday? What the hell? I could have gone with you or something."

He shakes his head. "I didn't really want to go anyway; not a big fan of heights. But would you be able to? Maybe send a picture or two to say I did it?"

I pull out my phone. "Yeah, yeah. I'll send the picture now then work on some more info when I'm on the train."

He lets out a sigh. "Thank you. Then I can get everything else done here and be in Paris tomorrow afternoon."

I feign shock. "*You'll* be in Paris next? *I'll* be in Paris next! What a coincidence!"

He kisses me, his lips lingering just long enough to borderline PDA. "I'll see you in Paris, Miss West."

"I'll see you in Paris Mr..." I look to the floor, searching for the name. "Am I forgetting this or have you still not told me your last name?"

"I have not told you my last name." Rocky's voice is very matter-of-fact.

I look at him, giving a nervous chuckle. "Intentionally?"

"Intentionally."

The weird feeling is suddenly back. It's one thing for it to be some silly fluke that happens in a sitcom or something, but it is completely different that he has *intentionally* withheld his full name from me.

"Rocky. What is your last name?" My voice has lost all humor.

"Promise me that nothing changes once I tell you." His face is sincere, but I am really creeped out.

"I can't promise that. I mean, what if you're on the FBI's most-wanted list or something? Things would definitely change. I'm obviously going to Google you now. Just tell me your fucking last name, Rocky." I hold my breath. Why is this such a big deal for him?

He lets out a sigh. "You won't have to Google it. My last name is Adams."

The fuck does he mean I won't have to Google it? Rocky Adams is not a name I've heard before. *Rocky Adams... Robert Adams... Jr...*

"Oh my God."

I place my purse down on one of my mom's barstool chairs and sling my coat over the back. She's in the living room, feet up on her coffee table wearing her thick slipper-socks. "Just in time! Bob's in Florence. Come see what you want to do when we're there."

The TV is paused on the title screen: "Bob Adams' Adventures in Florence." I lean over the back of the couch and kiss the top of my mom's head. "I thought I was just in charge of planning Paris."

"You are, but you're not just going to do what I want to do for almost two weeks. I want to know some stuff you would be interested in. Ready?" She holds the remote up, her finger hovering over the play button.

"Just a sec. I'm going to get some water. Need anything while I'm up?"

"I'll take a water, too—still water," she adds, throwing back to the text she sent me the other night about making sure to order flat water if we don't want sparkling at restaurants.

I roll my eyes. She doesn't even have sparkling water in the house. She doesn't like carbonation. I fill up two glasses of water and stand by her legs, waiting for her to put them down so I can squeeze by.

"Would you mind stepping over?"

"Mom, not again. Are they numb?" I step over, barely keeping my water from spilling all over the both of us.

"It's fine. I'm fine." She reassures me. "I went to the doctor and he said that my circulation just isn't what it once was."

I stare at her for a bit. She doesn't like going to the doctor alone.

"Don't look at me like that. It was one of those video calls. I knew you would be too busy to go with me."

"Mom, I think this is something you should go in and get checked out. Make an appointment. I can take the day off work to take you."

She waves me away with her hand. "To Florence!" She presses play and the familiar theme starts. At the last few notes, we sing along in unison. We've been watching Bob Adams for years. Well, she has. I have had it playing as background noise throughout my entire childhood.

This episode looks more recent—not brand new, but pretty close. The recording doesn't have the grainy quality some of the first episodes have. Bob takes us through some of the major tourist attractions—some church, a museum, the usual—but I am on my phone throughout, scrolling social media.

About halfway through the episode, Mom pauses and asks, "Alright, what is one thing you'd want to see?"

I shrug. "I don't know. The statue of David? I guess?"

She takes out a piece of paper and scribbles something down, chuckling to herself, before resuming the episode.

My eyes are still on my phone, but I hear Bob in the background, "And as a special treat, we meet up with my son for dinner. He is in Florence for a semester abroad and wants to show us his favorite spot for pasta."

"He's cute," my mom cuts in.

I glance at the screen. The guy is like a young version of Bob, but a little less geeky-looking. Mind you, I said a *little* less. They are seated at a table outside under a canopy, eating pasta and drinking wine.

"We'll have to be careful about wine with you. They put it in a lot of their foods."

"I'll survive, Mom. It's just hives. Besides, it's not like I'm going to down glasses of red."

"Hives in the heat of summer? I'd hate it." She keeps her eyes on the screen. "No, but he is *really* cute. I bet he's about your age."

I look again. He is kind of cute. "He's been traveling the world since he was in diapers. I bet he's a pretentious snob."

My mom all but clutches her pearls. "*Bob* is not pretentious, and I doubt he would raise his kids to be. He probably has a love for adventure and travel. Whisk you off to exotic locales for a weekend date. Besides, he's the son of public television royalty. He probably gets loads of perks."

I can't help but laugh. "I don't think that's how public television works, Mom."

"What do you think he's doing now? This episode is a few years old, so he's probably graduated and has a job. Something in international relations. Oh! Some sort of representative to Italy for a Fortune 500 company."

"Sure, Mom."

"I bet he did crew. He has the build for crew."

"What, like rowing? He probably has the money for it..."

"Say what you will, but I think you two would be a cute match."

"Whatever you say, Mom."

The episode ends with a view over the entire city and my mom points at the screen. "There. I want to see that view." She scribbles down another note on her paper.

"Please just say something," Rocky pleads.

I guess I was a bit lost in thought. "...and you just *kept* that from me? That your dad is Bob Adams?"

"Yes. I did. It was really nice to get to know someone without me being Bob Adams' kid."

"And all the times we've talked about the guidebook, you didn't once think to bring up, 'Hey, that's my father?'" I'm almost yelling at this point.

"Of course I did. I was going to tell you eventually." He gestures between us. "Obviously, I just did. I just wanted you to like *me*. Not who I work for or who I'm related to."

I jab my finger in his chest. "That's another thing. You said he was your boss. I knew you were holding something back yesterday, but, once again, I trusted you."

He grabs my hand, trying to hold it in both of his. "He *is* my boss. I edit for his guidebooks. He wants me to learn the trade, maybe take over for him one day."

I pull away. "It just feels so...disingenuous." I look him up and down. The resemblance is uncanny. How I couldn't see it before is beyond me. He looks just like his dad, just a little less nerdy. "What were you trying to get out of not telling me who you were? What did you have to gain from this little game?"

"My last girlfriend never loved me." Rocky bites his lips together, thinking, probably trying to concoct another half-truth. "It was two years into the relationship, when she rejected my proposal, that the truth came out. After the breakup, her friends let me know that she started dating me and stayed with me for free trips."

I stare at him. Sure, it sounds plausible, but it doesn't excuse the blatant secrecy.

"Lisa, I'm sorry. I didn't realize it would be this important to you. I was just enjoying knowing that you liked me for me."

Tears welling in my eyes, I look at my watch. Ten minutes until my train leaves. I look back to Rocky, my voice catching in my throat. "I did like you for you." I reach into my bag and pull out my itinerary for Paris. "I'm going to go to Paris and I am going to follow the itinerary I wrote for myself. I am not sure we will be crossing paths again, so..." I take a deep, stuttering breath. "Goodbye."

"Goodbye." Rocky's voice is a whisper, almost lost in the noise of the crowd.

I rush to my platform, almost unable to see through the tears in my eyes. I make it in time, store my bag, and plop down into my seat. Anger controls my thoughts for the first half hour of the ride—a feeling of betrayal, almost. How the hell could he just gloss over who his dad was? We'd talked about his parents, about his family. About how they went to Europe a lot, how they worked in the travel industry. He couldn't just *mention* that he happened to be the son of one of America's foremost authorities on international travel?

Slowly, as I come down from my seething, I start to sympathize. It was probably tough living life being the son of someone recognizable. Maybe not as bad as being a Kardashian's kid or something, but still an expectation would be there. And the story about his last girlfriend? If that were true, I could understand him being hesitant.

But he should have trusted me. He asked me to trust him so much, but he couldn't do the same for me? I mean, obviously I'm not some bitch who would string him along for a couple trips to the Mediterranean.

Bolting through the French countryside, I finally realize that my anger was my out. This relationship needed to end, and doing it in Geneva just allows me to get back to my normal life sooner. I needed a reason to cut ties. This was it. As bad as I feel for blowing up at him, it will hopefully be a clear end to the fling. Because that is all it was.

I pull out my phone and draft a few paragraphs in a text to Rocky about the cathedral, the prices, and the view. Once I hit send, I follow it up with another message.

> Lisa: I'm sorry for blowing up at you. It was a shock and I felt you should have been able to trust me. I'd say we are okay, but I still think we should just do our own thing in Paris.

I watch a few towns come and go out my window before I get his response.

Rocky: I really am sorry. If I had known you'd be this hurt, I would have told you sooner. I'm glad we're okay. Have a good rest of your trip.
Rocky: And thanks for the notes. I ended up being able to make it after all, though. Great view. A little high up, though.

I tuck my phone away. *I guess that's it.* There ends my summer fling.

A food and beverage cart comes around, offering complimentary lunch and beer or wine because *apparently* my mom booked first class for this train journey. I hadn't even realized until now, but I guess that explains why it is so quiet and comfy. I get a sandwich and a beer. As I eat, I take a look at my itinerary, typed and printed.

Day 11
Train to Paris: TGV Lyria 10:29am, Confirmation: JKL69
Arrive Paris Gare de Lyon 1:42pm
Hotel Confirmation: ASDF420, Double twin room
Metro 1 to Palais Royal stop
3:00 Tickets to Louvre, Barcode in Confirmation Email
Walk down the Champs-Élysées, see Arc de Triomphe if time
Dinner: See Food and Drink map in Bob Adams, p. 134, choose from highlighted

See the Eiffel Tower light up after sunset
(8:56pm)
RER C back to hotel

See, Mom? THAT is an itinerary. Time-stamped, everything organized in one place. Knowing exactly where I am going and what I am doing... Except... I open *Bob Adams' Adventures* to p. 134 and select a bistro near the Louvre, scribbling it down next to "Dinner." Smiling to myself, I realize one more thing. The bank I transferred funds to has a branch near the Champs-Élysées, so I will go there instead of walking all the way to the Arc de Triomphe. Easy peasy.

I settle into my chair, knowing nothing can go wrong now. As long as I stick to my itinerary, everything will fall into place in Paris.

We arrive at a massive train station, probably the busiest I've seen so far on this trip. Even finding the exit is a trek, as it looks like some spaces are blocked off for construction of some kind. I have to leave the building and then enter another part of the building before I can actually see the exit to the street. My hotel isn't far, but pushing through the throngs of people makes me realize that Paris is a dense city, especially compared to Geneva.

The hotel is so peaceful compared to the bustle just outside the door. It takes a while for the line of people to get checked in, but I just keep reading my book on my phone while I wait. It's getting pretty good. In an effort to save time, I don't even try to check in using my French. Maybe I'll practice later.

I leave my bags with bell services and take just my small bag with my *Bob Adams*, my printed itinerary, a few snacks, my passport, and a sweater. I put my passport inside the guidebook and the sweater on top of everything so if someone finds their hand in my bag, it will be harder to steal the last piece of identification I have left.

On the metro, I find myself wearing my bag in front of me, both hands covering it. My innate trust in others has been pretty shaken, apparently. Nobody around me seems to care, though. Everyone is doing their own thing for the most part. I glance at the books some people are reading, but I can't make out their titles well enough to look them up for myself. I probably couldn't do a whole book in French, anyway.

I make it to the Louvre with some time to spare, so I walk around the perimeter. The building is massive, and the glass pyramid in the middle seems both out-of-place and perfectly situated. Despite having pre-bought tickets, I still have to wait in line for a while before I can enter. But once I'm in, wow. Just wow. *This* is what an art museum should look like. Massive rooms with great works well-spaced on every wall. Crowds of people move from painting to painting efficiently. I get a glimpse of the Mona Lisa—shout out to a fellow Lisa, I guess—but from my vantage point, it looks about as big as a postage stamp. There is no way to get closer. It seems like that is the only thing a bunch of people are here to see. Well, that and Venus de Milo. I try to strike her pose, but I get a cramp in my back contorting like that. Besides, what am I supposed to do with my arms?

The pieces that draw me in most, though, are the Iznik tiles in the Islamic Gallery. The ceramic pieces are adorned with bright, beautiful hand-painted colors, so well-preserved and bringing brightness to this darkened room. I stare at them for quite some time, getting lost in the flowers and patterns. Perhaps my next trip will be to somewhere further east, where these kinds of things were created. I shake the idea. I'm not sure I'll ever get to go on an adventure like this one again.

I manage a sighting of a Monet piece in the French painting area. Maybe it's a little basic, but he's my favorite painter. His colors and the fuzziness of the impressionist style really draw me in, but the one I see here is a winter scene along a river—there is no brightness to it at all. Part of me feels let down, but I know I'll get to see the Water Lilies the day after tomorrow, so not all is lost.

I stay at the museum as long as I can, but employees start ushering people out a little before six. I feel like I barely got to see anything here, and as I walk out I try to steal glances at a few last pieces. It seems my interest in museums has been rekindled. Probably from that restorative trip to the lake. Damn Rocky for being right.

I do have to race through a pretty huge park to make it to the bank before they close, but I barely squeeze in. Good thing I decided against stopping at the ice cream cart near that fountain. After convincing the teller that I only need one piece of identification, since I have the police report that my other ID was stolen, I walk out with a giant wad of euros tucked in three separate spots—a third of it in my travel guide, a third in my sweater pocket, and a third in my sock, save a few in my front pocket to pay for dinner.

After walking past a bunch of stores that are way too expensive for me, even if I do have about half of my savings on me in cash, I head to the bistro I picked out before and get a spot outside. The weather isn't too unbearable, and since I spent the hottest part of the day inside, I feel like I can handle a bit of sun. Despite having a sandwich for lunch, I order a croque madame for dinner. Yes, that is a sandwich for two meals in a row, but this one is warm and has an egg on top...so...that's different enough, right? My mom wouldn't judge me for it. In fact, she'd probably be having one right along with me, while also popping some probiotic pills to "offset the salmonella" that she would be convinced is in the runny egg.

Street lights start to flicker on one at a time and it's almost like I can see the electric current as it courses down the avenue. I take it as my cue to make my way toward the tower. At first, I dread what looks to be almost a half-hour walk, but once I make it to the river, I realize that I will be able to see the whole show from here.

Standing along the concrete wall, I watch tour boats pass by on the river below. Exhausted kids rest their heads on their parents' laps. Along the river bank below, other tourists seem to be waiting for the same spectacle. I spot a couple, hands clasped, pressed against each other, stealing kisses every few minutes. Out of the corner of my eye, I see the flickering added to the solid lights on the landmark. A gasp erupts along the river, followed by "oohs" and "ahhs" echoing off the bank opposite.

My heart hurts as I long for someone to share this with. My mom would have loved it. She'd probably have us wearing berets and chomping baguettes while it happens, just to be extra, but it would have been a blast. The tower shimmers and a family next to me turns around for a group selfie. I realize I should probably do the same. I force a smile, hoping it doesn't show how sad I actually am. The moment the shutter clicks, the grief hits like a train and I start to cry right then and there.

I want my mom. I want to be on the trip she wanted to take with me.

I want to go home, honestly. But if I do go home, it won't be *home*. Home is where my mom drops by every week to watch whatever show we're binging together. Home is where my dad comes to help with a leaky sink or a broken heart.

I need to do this somewhere private. People are staring. I could try to take the metro back, but I can't get a hold of myself. I can barely get a breath in between sobs. I pull out my phone and request a rideshare. The wait isn't long. The poor driver seems very concerned and asks if I'm alright, but I can't slow my breathing enough to speak.

I manage to eke out some words to get my key and retrieve my bags at the front desk so I can bring them up to my room. Once I'm in my room, I push my rolling bag across the floor and I throw myself against the door and slide down, bawling. It seems very dramatic, but I *feel* dramatic.

I am an orphan.

I am alone in Paris.

All I have left in the world is my sister, but she is busy with her own family. I take out my phone to call her, but realize that she is probably at work. Instead, I send her the picture of me in front of the Eiffel Tower.

Keeping my phone out, I play the next episode of Downton Abbey, but it's one about a baby not having a mother anymore and I have to turn it off almost immediately. Instead, I take out my fantasy novel. Surprise, surprise, it is revealed that her dad was murdered less than four pages into my reading. It takes all my strength to not throw my phone across the room.

Somehow I find my way to the bed and lie down, my head facing the other bed—what was supposed to be my mom's bed—still perfectly made. I hate this. I hate this so much.

Chapter 14

Is there such a thing as a sadness hangover? I'm definitely past the active wave of grief, but I still feel the hurt lingering in my blood. I want to throw up, but I know it won't help. The bed is my only comfort right now, so I lie in it a little while longer as the clock ticks on.

My tickets for Versailles are for 10:15. To get there on time, I need to leave around nine. ... *Wait. Is that right?* I roll over to the other side of the bed and pull out my itinerary.

Day 12
RER C from Austerlitz to Versailles-Chantiers, 9:03 am
Versailles 10:15 am, ticket printed (PDF on cloud storage)
Lunch in Versailles (Mom's choice)
Return to Paris RER C
Seine River Dinner Cruise 7:00 pm

I peek at my phone. 8:45 am. *Shit.* I bolt out of bed and throw on whatever I can. Thankfully I planned ahead and can just whip my Versailles tickets out of my documents folder. I am tying my shoes as I wait for the elevator, my sweater only on one arm at this point. I can't miss this train. If I miss the train, I might not make it to the palace in time. Not only would I lose out on the cost of the tickets, but I'd also miss the one palace in Europe I actually *wanted* to see.

When I hit the lobby, the front desk has no line. I pop over to see how fruitless my efforts might be.

"Can I make it to the Austerlitz station by 9:03?"

The woman at the front desk squints and shakes her head. "You might, but Austerlitz is closed this week for maintenance. You will have to use the next station."

My heart drops. "Do you know any other way I can get to Versailles by 10:15?"

"Taxi? Rideshare, maybe?"

I pull out my phone. A few taps later, I find that the only way I am going to make it on time is to leave right now and pay eighty euros for a rideshare. I groan but force a smile as I turn back to the front desk attendant. "Thank you."

"Good luck," I hear her say as I scurry out of the front doors.

My car is on the other side of the street, but he is gesturing for me to cross. It's not a crosswalk, and there isn't even a sidewalk on that side. I gesture my response, indicating there are cars coming and there is nowhere for me to cross. He gestures toward the red light in front of him, at which point I notice the large sign indicating he is not allowed to U-turn. The light turns green and his eyes go wide. There's a small break in the cars so I book it across and hop in, the door closing right as my driver starts moving, nearly avoiding hitting a median pole. Well, if I wasn't awake before, I am now.

The drive out is long and slow—this must be Paris rush hour. I wish I could nap, but I'm not so sure about falling asleep in a stranger's car. Instead, I pull out *Bob Adams' Adventures* and read up on the palace and gardens I am about to visit. I brush up on my French history until I start to get a bit of a headache from reading in the car. After that, I set my book on the seat next to me and just stare out the window, listening to whatever the driver has on the radio—a mix of songs in French and English. The English ones are *not* censored. The first few curse words take me by surprise, but eventually, I realize the words clearly do not carry the same weight over here.

I am dropped off right in front of the palace next to a huge statue. A smattering of people dot the large courtyard trying to sell tourists bottled beverages, umbrellas, and Paris-themed tchotchkes. *Umbrellas?* I look up and realize for the first time that it is overcast. It might even rain by the looks of it.

The line to get in is shockingly long. A woman walks up and down it, yelling in four languages that you should only be in the line if your ticketed entry time is within thirty minutes. Mine is in five, so I join it. It isn't a stop-and-start type of line, but rather a continuous, slow shuffle toward a beautiful golden gate where it turns to the entry door. The real bottleneck is where people are pausing by the gate for a selfie. As angry as I am with all of the people slowing down the line, I still take a second to get a shot of myself in front of the gate. Hypocritical? Possibly. But the selfie is super cute, so it's worth it.

Versailles is...incredible. Tour groups swarm around certain views and rooms, trying their best to squeeze their phones into the perfect shot—the chapel, the queen's bedroom, certain paintings. I take my phone out for quick snaps of every picture that has a dog chilling in the bottom corner because they're pretty tops, but everything else is enjoyed using the lens of my eyeball instead.

I come upon a room mostly void of people, everyone just assuming it's a hallway, I guess. But there are a few stairs on the right that I take, leading me through the arches and up to statues of beautiful women. Naked, powerful women representing the seasons and the elements, the night and the hunt. I stop to look at each one bathed in the light coming in from the massive windows that look out onto the garden. I want so badly to reach out and touch them. Nothing is stopping me from doing it, and there are no guards in sight, but my impulsive thoughts lose this battle.

Just as I start to feel pinned in by the endless tourists and narrow walkways through rooms, I come to what I think is the end, until I remember that my ticket includes entrance into the gardens. A quick stroll before lunch sounds delightful, so I make my way downstairs to yet *another* line for entry. This one is pretty quick, and I get a chance to look over the map before I make it through the turnstile. It is only when I get my bearings and find a recognizable landmark on the map that I realize the scale—this will be no quick stroll. These gardens are *massive*. People are renting golf carts to get around out here. French royalty were really out here living well. I mean...until the end. I rub my neck and move on, starting through a circular path through hedges and roses.

The fresh air and space are a welcome escape. Beautifully manicured plants and shrubs fill every glance. Down some stairs and along a field, I come across hedges so tall I can't even see through them. Winding my way in, I find fountains, trees, and statues, all in their own little areas. This is a museum all its own. Just when I am about to pull out the map to figure out where I am, I come across some restrooms that almost look like a little house hidden away among the trees. After a considerable wait in line, I find that my birth control *did* work. *Shit.* Yay for not being pregnant, but shit for knowing that my period might be coming today but being in too much of a hurry this morning to remember to pack any hygiene products.

Time to test my French, I guess.

Sitting on my toilet, I holler. "Excusez-moi. Avez-vous un...pad? ...ou un tampon?" Not sure pad is the correct term, but tampon sounds French as-is, right? I finally remember the word for *anyone* and throw that in helplessly, "...quelqu'un?"

"Où êtes-vous?" a voice asks.

I stare at the door. There is no space below for me to wiggle my fingers out. This is great for privacy, but not so great for handing menstrual products between stalls. Instead, I have to open the door a crack, my shorts still around my ankles, and stick my hand out. After waving it once or twice, a pad is pressed into my palm. "Merci beaucoup!" When I bring it back in, I can see it is a huge, bulky one, but I don't have any right to complain. At least I'm not going to be bleeding through my shorts. Thank goodness for the universal tradition of girls helping girls.

Leaving the restroom, I find a little restaurant, just hidden away in the trees. My stomach growls on cue. I haven't eaten yet today and I haven't even seen half of the gardens yet. I should probably restore some energy before moving on.

A sandwich and ice cream bar in a picturesque garden patio later, I finish my rounds. There are so many little secret areas tucked into labyrinths of shrubs. I end up back at the palace, so sure I have seen everything, yet when I look at the map, I find new places. My watch tells me it is time to leave if I'm going to have time to change before the river cruise tonight. I make my way back to the front, making a quick detour through the gift shop, picking out some trinkets for my sister. My rideshare request is picked up immediately. I look up to find the car is right in front of me, letting their last passengers out.

The driver is so much more talkative than the last few I've had, which is nice, because going through that entire palace with nobody to bounce ideas off of was less than ideal. And maybe I was just a little lonely. Once he clocks that I'm American, he asks if he can practice his English. I agree, but only if I can practice French. In our respective broken second languages, we talk about Versailles, about Paris, and about some of the more interesting characters he's had in his back seat. I don't even think to glance at my phone, as he keeps me engaged the whole time. His English is much better than my French, and sometimes I have to dip back into English since my French vocabulary is desperately lacking for the deeper conversations we get into.

By the time we approach the hotel, I almost don't want to get out, but this ride is already pretty pricey so I decide it is probably for the best. Five stars plus a huge tip.

After a quick shower to freshen up, I find texts from my sister.

> Alice: What time can I video call you today? I need to make sure you're still alive.
> Alice: The twins are home with a cold, so it can be any time. I would love to think about anything other than snot for a few minutes.

It's five pm. Dinner cruise starts at seven. Dinner cruise...for two...in Paris. *Oh, shit.*

> Lisa: Want to be my dinner date? I'll prop you up on the wine glass across from me or something.
> Alice: What time?
> Lisa: I think it would be like one, but the dinner is the second half of the trip, so maybe 1:30 or 2?
> Alice: Deal. But pop me on for some sightseeing, too. I want to see the Eiffel Tower.
> Lisa: You'd see all the monuments if you were here.
> Alice: Well, I'm sorry for having children right between Dad and Mom dying. Maybe be mad at them for choosing a bad time to die instead.

> Lisa: Oh, I am mad at them. I'll tell you all about
> Mom's shitty itinerary.

I half feel bad about that last text, but Mom would blame everything on Dad when he wasn't around to defend himself anymore. Never in a mean way, always joking. Finding humor wherever she could in widowhood. I could always tell she missed him, though.

I miss them both.

I get dolled up in my nicest dress, realizing I am quickly running out of clean clothes. At least I only have a few more days to go. I put on some makeup, too, remembering that this was supposed to be my mom's and my fancy day in Paris—a palace and a glamorous night cruise. I can still hear her laugh, like she's in the corner helping me get ready for prom, gossiping about the boys at my school.

But when her ghost disappears, the room is actually silent, save for the noise of the traffic outside.

My lip gloss applicator hovers over my lip as I'm holding back the grief once more. This is the point where Rocky rescues me, right? This is when something bad happens and he rushes in to save the day. He could be arriving by train at any moment now, just a block or two away.

But no, we are done. There is no Paris chapter to our story. Paris is for me alone. For me. Alone.

I dab my lips together and plop everything back into my toiletry bag, giving myself one more look-over before leaving for the river. The pick-up point isn't too far from the hotel, so I walk along the bank, my feet protesting the heeled ankle boots I keep forcing them into. I can spot the boat a bridge away, blue lights illuminating it from the inside. I join a line down a gangway filled with couples.

When I get to the front, the man working scans my ticket, then looks behind me. "Is this your date?" He points to a man in line behind me, who is clearly holding hands with another woman, who pulls him closer.

"No." I point at my phone. "This is my date."

He blinks a few times. "It is only you?"

I give a pressed-lip smile. "Only me."

He doesn't say anything else, but waves me through, turning his attention to my not-date and his girlfriend.

The blue light radiates from the windows of the floor below, but this top level is still warm with the sun's midsummer evening glow. A waiter walks around with glasses of champagne, offering one to me.

"Sorry, I'm allergic."

"For your date, then?"

"Sorry, I'm alone."

He leaves wordlessly, his eyes wide, as if the two biggest sins in France are being allergic to wine and being alone. Maybe I should have invited Rocky. Or *maybe* I should be a strong, badass woman who is comfortable with her own company.

I like the idea of the second one better, but at the same time, I think I should have done something to thank Rocky for making this trip a little less miserable. Finding a spot at the railing, I pull out my phone and start a message.

Lisa: Hey, thanks again for—

I stop and erase my message. This is over. He kept some pretty big information from me. But it doesn't stop me from thinking about him and how nice it would be to have him next to me as we creep down the Seine, looking up at the bridges and monuments. As the sun sinks down lower, lights start to flicker on, illuminating the city in a warm glow. At this point, I call my sister, popping in an earbud so we're not distracting everyone else on the boat.

"Hey, ugly," I greet.

"Well, that's unfortunate, because everyone always said I'm prettier than you," Alice quips back.

I shrug. "That's why you're married and I'm not."

"Or it could be because I'm an old woman while you are but a child."

I switch to the forward-facing camera, putting the Eiffel Tower into frame. "Look. A tower."

"I thought it would be more...flashy."

"Oh, the flashy is pretty, but I don't know if we'll be nearby when it turns on again."

"Want to see my view for the day?" Alice flips her camera, showing me two babies sitting up, snot pouring down their upper lips.

"Ew. Little germ factories."

"Excuse me?"

"Cute little germ factories. *Adorable* little germ factories."

"Oh, yeah, no. They're disgusting." She changes her pitch to a cutesy baby voice. "And pretty soon Mommy's going to be disgusting, too, huh? Because you can't just keep those viruses to yourself. And work will be mad again because I've missed too many days this year." Her voice goes back to normal. "I can't believe your work let you take all this time off. Do you have to do any work remotely?"

"No. I even signed out of my work email on my phone. They were really nice about it."

"Oh! Show me that statue!" Alice's face comes back on the screen.

I point the phone up toward the statue on the bridge we are floating under.

"Wow, that is fucking magical." She pauses for a minute, soaking in the view. "So tell me about this itinerary. Was it all super lame stuff?"

"No, it was pretty cool, but it was more bullet points than an actual itinerary. There was no schedule, no pre-booked stuff—except a car from the airport that I completely missed—it was all loosey-goosey."

"Ah, and my wound-up sister couldn't handle it?"

"I tried. I really did. But I was relieved when I finally got to Paris and had everything organized the way I liked it."

"Seven fifty-five am, open eyes. Seven fifty-five and ten seconds, remove covers from body."

"Ha. Ha. Ha." I add some extra length between each *ha* to emphasize my lack of amusement. "No. But at least I know where I'm going to eat for the most part. Have you ever tried to figure out food in a foreign country when you're already cranky from hunger and wine is hidden in everything? It's rough."

"Oh, poor girl, eating delicious foods in a foreign country."

We joke around a bit more as we look at the sights, but then I'm called down to dinner. Both water glasses are full, so I rest

Alice against one of them. The twins are down for a nap, so she makes herself a peanut butter and jelly sandwich and places it in front of her, resting me on whatever toy is on their dining table.

My first course comes—a light salad. I can see the waiter holding back a comment about the phone on the table, but when I dare him to with my eyes, he just leaves.

"You know, I almost wanted to invite Rocky to this. As great as you are as a date, at least he would be physically *here*."

Alice pushes the glob of sandwich to her cheek. "Wait. The guy you met in Rome is in Paris now?"

"Oh my gosh, I haven't told you any of this yet?"

She sits forward. "Any of what? Spill."

"Yeah, no. Mom planned our trip based on a recommended itinerary in her *Bob Adams' Adventures* book. Rocky did the same one, just a day off. He's been in every city I have, just a day later."

"Oh my gosh, that's adorable! Did you meet up in every city?"

"Almost. I was only in Florence for a day, but I did see him at the train station."

"And you two went on more dates, right...?" Her eyebrows wiggle a bit.

I roll my eyes. "Yes."

"And you got some?"

I narrow my eyes.

"I'll take that as a yes, then. I have to ask, though—you used protection, right?"

I look around, making sure nobody heard, until I realized she's still in my earbud. "Yes. I'm on the pill," I hiss.

Her face falls flat. "I was on the pill when my two crotch goblins happened."

"You were also on antibiotics," I remind her. "And besides, I'm on my period now. We're good."

"Ah, is that why there's no date with Rocky tonight?"

"No. He was withholding information from me."

"Like, he's married?"

"No. Just who he is."

"A murderer?" Alice perks up. She adores those true crime podcasts.

"No. Get this. His name is Robert Adams."

"Yeah, so he's super...white?"

"What's the nickname for Robert?"

"Rob?"

"The other nickname."

"Bob?"

"Yeah."

"I don't get it."

I roll my eyes. "Bob Adams, like the guidebooks."

"Oh, so he's old!" Her brow furrows. "I mean, whatever floats your boat, I guess. How did you not recognize him, though? Mom watched that show all the time."

"It's his kid. Rocky is Bob Adams' son."

"Okay, so he is well-traveled? I'm still not sure what the issue is here."

"He didn't tell me, Alice. For over a week we went out and spent nights together, but he never told me his last name because—" I realize how loud my voice is getting and bring it back down to a near-whisper, "—he didn't want me to know who he was."

Alice's face melts. "And that really hurt you, huh?"

My eyes start to well with tears. "It did. After telling him so many times that he looked familiar, he just brushed it off. He had so many chances to tell me."

Her eyes light up. "You really like him."

"What? Did you not hear me? He basically lied to me."

"Yeah, I heard you, but you wouldn't be this hurt unless you *really* liked him. Did he tell you *why* he didn't tell you earlier?"

"He said one of his last girlfriends just stayed with him for travel benefits basically. He wanted me to know him outside of the context of his dad."

"And that wasn't a good enough explanation for you?"

I stop making eye contact with the phone. "I guess not? I mean, I can see why he did it, but I still feel like he should have trusted me."

"Trusted you more than a girlfriend he dated for more than a week and a half?"

"Alice, I blew up at him the last time I saw him. I was so angry. I don't think there's any coming back from that. Besides, he's from Chicago. And his work has him in Europe for long periods. It's not like this was going to go anywhere, anyway."

"Why not? You like him. You don't get this emotional over guys, Lees. You're too in your head all the time. I think this guy might have reached somewhere else."

I glare at her.

"Ugh, I'm being serious. Not your vagina. Your *heart.*" She shrugs, taking another bite of her sandwich. "Yeah, but I guess your vagina, too."

"*Beep. Battery low,*" My earbud yells. Thankfully it didn't die right before my sister said vagina.

"Hey, Alice. My headphones are about to die. Thanks for keeping me company, though."

"Alright, little sis. I guess I'll go change the sheet in the Pack N Play. It's *drenched* in mucus."

The waiter sets down my main course right as she says that. "Thanks. That image is just what I need for this course with a strange jelly on it."

She gives me a salute. "I do what I can. Love ya."

"Love you, too." I hit the end button and pull out my earbud, revealing the music of the band that had appeared sometime during the first course. The rest of the dinner, I keep thinking about Rocky. Maybe it wasn't a fling. Maybe I had actually fallen for him. All I want now is to call him, to make plans, but I already ended it. And despite what my sister says, his living in another part of the country *does* put a wrench in attempting a relationship. It just wouldn't work.

My heart bounces back and forth between texting him and not. I decide to wait until tomorrow since tonight is about strong, independent womanhood. After dessert, some couples take a romantic spin around the dance floor, but that is a step too far for me. No way I'm going to go up there and slow dance by myself. Instead, I watch the couples, my eyes lingering on two women who just seem so lost in each other—like nothing else in the world exists. They probably have loads of problems waiting for them in the real world, but right in this moment, it's just them. It's beautiful.

I head straight back to the hotel once we dock. It's pretty late and I'm hoping to get to the Eiffel Tower right as it opens to get in before the masses. A good night's sleep will be to my benefit. Plus, if I'm up early enough I might even get to enjoy an authentic Parisian breakfast. My mouth waters at the thought of a fresh croissant as I nod off to sleep.

Chapter 15

It doesn't take me long to find a place that sells croissants, but I am pretty wary when most people in line are speaking English. It just doesn't feel...right. So I wind down a few more streets, further from the train station, and stumble upon a place with a line literally out the door, locals buzzing on about this, that, and the other while waiting. The buttery smell wafting from the front door seals the deal, so I join the queue.

Boy howdy, was I right in waiting. Best croissant I've ever had in my entire life. Thankfully, I bought three. Maybe it's overkill, but one had chocolate and one had almonds, so I couldn't justify *not* trying them all. The almond is my favorite. Or maybe it's the chocolate. Or maybe the classic plain? I don't know—they are all fantastic. I nibble on each in turn as I walk over a bridge and a few blocks more to the metro stop that will take me to the Eiffel Tower, stuffing the leftovers in my bag for later snacking.

Once on the subway, I pull out today's itinerary.

Day 13
Metro 6 from Quai de la Gare to Bir-Hakeim
Eiffel Tower (opens 9:30am)
Lunch (see p. 133 Bob Adams, restaurants near

Eiffel Tower)
Walk to Museum, ~35 min
Musée de l'Orangerie (Water Lilies!) - tickets for
2:00 pm
Dinner at hotel
Pack for trip home

Even though I'm there almost an hour before opening, the security line is already massive. Peddlers lay out blankets to sell little Eiffel Tower keychains and statuettes, approaching people as their spot in line passes by. I keep an ear out for the lowest price someone pays for one, in case I want to get one later, so I'll know how low I can try to get.

Once I'm through the security line, there's another line for tickets. I knew I should have pre-booked this, but they didn't sell tickets to the top when I was planning a few months ago.

The line snakes around a few times, with kids trying to swing from the stanchions, one knocking them over a few times. I, too, am pretty bored. I take out my phone. *I should text him…* I open our messages only to see three dots. Then they disappear. I type out a few nonsense letters, then erase them. Let him know I'm there, too. The dots don't reappear, so I tuck my phone away. Maybe he was trying to message someone else and realized it was the wrong person mid-message.

A few more zigs and zags bring me to the front of the line. I pay for my ticket then immediately enter another, albeit shorter, line to get to the elevator. The ride to the first level is…strange. The angle of the elevator is unsettling. Thankfully the next one will be more vertical. I feel my phone buzz when we're partway up, but we're crammed in there like sardines, so I decide to wait until we're off to check my message. It's not a message, though, I realize as it keeps ringing. Someone is *calling* me. *Who the hell calls someone...? Unless...* I dig it out of my bag. It's Rocky.

"Hello?"

"Hi, uh..." It's not Rocky's voice. It's a woman. "This man doesn't seem to be doing so well and when I asked if I could help him, he handed me his phone as it was calling you." She is almost shouting over a noise behind her that I can't place.

My heart sinks. "Oh my God, is Rocky okay?"

I hear her voice go quieter. "Rocky? Is that your name, honey?" It increases in volume. "Yeah. I think he's just scared."

I panic, looking around to see if there's an exit. Obviously there's not. It's an elevator. "Where are you? I'll be there as soon as I can."

"We're at the top of the Eiffel Tower. He's pinned himself against a wall near the elevator, sitting on the ground. He's not saying anything, and will barely even look up at me. I think he might be afraid of heights."

I finally place the sound. It's the wind. "I'll be there as soon as I can. Would you mind waiting with him until I can get there? I'm about to get off the second-floor elevator now."

"I can do that, sweetie." Her voice gets quiet again. "Your friend is on her way here now. She's close. I'll wait with you until she gets here. You want to talk to her?" There's a long pause and some shuffling before I hear the woman's voice again. "He took the phone, but I don't think he can get any words out. Poor thing."

I push to be the first one off the elevator. "The line for the top floor elevator is pretty long. It might be a second."

"No worries." She moves the phone away once again. "Honey, you take the kids and get some good shots. I'll grab our champagne and come find you when we're done." She comes back to me. "I'll be here. We'll see you soon."

"Thank y—," I try to respond, but she's already hung up. My heart starts to race as my mind does the same—*why would Rocky come up here if he's afraid of heights? Why am I the first person he thought to call? Is it because he knew I was in Paris? That must be it.*

The line scooches forward. We could have fit more people on that elevator.

Why isn't he talking, though? He can't be that afraid. Then again, I'm not sure what kind of mental state I would have been in if Rocky hadn't helped me through the prison area of the Doge's Palace.

We move forward some more. The attendant cuts the line off right before me, but I push past, pointing at the person in front of me, pretending I'm with her group. This elevator ride is actually more unsettling than the first. Even though it is vertical, it is high. Like, *really* high. I start to feel a bit dizzy myself, and I am not even afraid of heights. Not to mention, it is taking *forever*. I count the time in the heartbeats I can hear in my head.

I can't weasel my way off first this time, instead I'm nearly the last one. At least the lack of crowd behind me gives me a bit of time to look for Rocky without being jostled around.

"Rocky!" I shout as he comes into view. He is right where the woman said he would be—sitting on the ground, tucked into the fetal position. I rush to him, kneeling down next to him. I thought he would look like a sickly disheveled mess, but instead, he looks totally normal, just a bit...empty. "Rocky, are you ok?"

He looks up at me, finding my eyes and fixating on them. He shakes his head. "It's too high."

I look over at the woman next to him. "Thank you so much. You go join your family. I'll help him from here."

She nods, giving a sympathetic smile, then heads up the stairs to the observation area, calling out to her family. "Adam? Kids?"

I sit down next to Rocky, tucking my knees to my chest, too. "Hey, the sooner you get down, the sooner this is over."

"It's the elevator." He pauses for some deep breaths. "This is because of the elevator. I haven't even looked out at the view because I couldn't make it that far."

"So the elevator is the problem, then." I sigh. "I take it the stairs are out of the picture, too?"

He turns to me, glaring.

I hold up my hands. "Not a joke. Legitimate question. I guess that's a no, though."

"No stairs. I just need help getting into the elevator and down."

I hold out my hand. "Let's do this."

He takes it with a shaking hand. It's still a strong grasp, still warm and comforting. I can only hope my hand feels the same to him.

I stand, pulling him up with me. His legs wobble. He looks ready to faint. "Just look at me. Watch me the whole way." I walk backward, pulling him along but still facing him. "Just watch me."

Rocky keeps his eyes on me, but they stray occasionally. When I give a cough, he snaps right back to my eyes.

There is hardly a line for going down the elevator—everyone seems to be enjoying the sights for now. When the elevator arrives, I pull Rocky toward it. He doesn't move at first.

"Rocky. Just trust me. Please."

He starts to look away.

"Rocky. My eyes are over here. Just follow me."

He nods and keeps his eyes on mine. I walk backward through the turnstile and into the elevator and Rocky slowly follows. I can hear his breathing speed up as the door closes. When the cabin lurches downward, he collapses, but I catch him on the way down, trying to hold him up with my body. "Rocky, just hang on to me. Just focus on me. Keep your eyes closed and just hold on."

He clutches me harder. I can feel his fingertips dig into my muscles. I rub his back. "Halfway there." It's really just a guess. My eyes are closed, too, trying to focus on the cues his body is giving me. His breath is stuttering. "Halfway there," I repeat in a whisper.

Soon enough, we're back to the second floor. "Do you want to take a break here or keep heading down?"

Rocky shakes his head. "I don't know. I want to be done but I don't want to do another elevator."

Time to make an executive decision. "Let's just get it over with, then." I pull him out of the elevator and guide him toward the line back down. This one will be a bit of a longer wait, it seems. I have to keep him distracted. "Hey, I'm sorry for yelling at you back in Geneva. It was just a lot, you know? And it hurt that you kept who you were from me for so long, especially when there were ample opportunities for you to tell me."

Rocky's face scrunches up. "Can we not talk about this?"

My chest tightens. "Yeah, okay."

"It's not that I don't *want* to talk about it, I just need to handle one thing at a time here, you know?"

"Yeah. Yeah, I get it. I'm just trying to keep you talking." It wasn't a total lie.

"And you thought that bringing up our fight was going to keep me talking?"

"Maybe? I don't know. I was so worried you didn't trust me, yet here you are calling me when you're not doing well and need some help."

"Lisa, not now." His skin is a ghostly shade of white. Perspiration collects at his hairline.

"Right. Right." I rock back and forth a bit. "How about that local sports team?"

"Do you actually want to know how PSG did last year and how they're looking this year or are you just trying to continue the conversation without knowing which topic to choose?"

I blink a few times. "The second one. I could not care less about Parisian sports."

He looks down at my hand. "Can I... Can I just...?" He holds it in his.

I interlace my fingers in his. "Yeah. You can."

We wait together in silence, staring down at our feet or our hands, not acknowledging that we drift closer and closer to the elevator. I guess he just needed me here. I glance over his shoulder to see a glimpse of the absolutely gorgeous view of the city. This is a good reason to miss out on it, though. I squeeze his hand a little tighter. He's not shaking anymore, but from time to time his whole body gives a shiver.

When it's finally our turn, we're crammed into the elevator with a crowd of other tourists. Rocky and I are pressed against each other, and when we look into each other's eyes, it's not desperate terror that fills them, but rather just an appreciation of being close to each other again. When the elevator begins its diagonal descent we grab onto each other. We don't clutch each other's torsos, though. I have a hold of his face and he has me around the waist. We pull each other in and kiss the whole ride down. Everyone else in the elevator be damned, I need to distract this man. And distract him I do. All the way to ground level.

When the elevator clears out, we stop. I bite my lip. Damn, that felt nice. I'm really hoping *that* wasn't our last kiss. The elevator attendant coughs to get our attention and we scurry out, fingers still linked. We make it out of the secure area and into a massive field nearby before either of us says anything. I have a thousand things to say, but I don't want to break the silence, so I just wait for him to go first.

"As horrible as that experience was, the last part was kind of nice."

I turn to him. "What the hell were you doing going up to the top of the Eiffel Tower if you're afraid of heights?" Oops. That was a yell. I suppose I'm a bit frustrated at the moment.

He looks confused for a second. "I... I have medication, but I forgot it at the hostel. I thought since I was fine at the cathedral in Geneva, I would be fine not going back to get it."

I gesture to the tower. "Does that look like a cathedral to you? Why did you even go up in the first place?"

He opens his mouth to speak, but then his eyes go wide. He turns and pukes in a nearby shrub. Glad he did that *after* I kissed him. He unslings his bag and hands me the camera from inside.

"Oh, shit. You needed pictures for work?"

"Yep. So now I have to go get my meds and go back up." His eyes follow the tower up, freezing on the top floor.

"No. You're going to go to your hostel and rest. Get that—" I gesture to the vomit plant, "—out of your system. I'll go see the view I came here for and get those pictures. What do you need?"

I can see there is something he wants to say but holds it back. "Uh...just some views from the top, some of the champagne bar, and maybe a couple pictures of the second floor, too."

"Right. Text me your hostel's name and your room number so I can drop this off when I'm done." I wave the camera around, getting a feel for it. I am not a photographer, but I can play one on TV. I turn to head back to the security line, but I feel Rocky's hand on my wrist.

"Lisa." He pulls me closer. "Just know that I *really* want to kiss you right now."

I press my lips together. "Brush your teeth first, then we'll talk."

He closes his eyes and nods. "Yep. Got it."

While in line for security a second time—this time for a much longer wait—I munch on what is left of the croissants from this morning. Apparently watching a grown man vomit in front of me could not take away my appetite. The ticket line, too, was obnoxiously long. I guess I had the right idea coming first thing in the morning. When I get to the front of the line, though, I find there are no more tickets to the top available today.

"No, I *need* to go to the top. I have to get pictures." When I see the ticket agent about to turn me down, I add. "It's for my boss. I work for Bob Adams."

She picks up a phone and dials a number, speaking in French that is too fast and too quiet for me to understand. When she hangs up, she does not speak immediately, but instead presses some keys on her computer. "I cannot give you elevator tickets to the top. You can buy the elevator to the second floor, then take the stairs to the top."

The fucking stairs. "Fine. Yes. I will do that." I grit my teeth for a moment before forcing out, "Thank you."

This time, I appreciate the elevator ride. I am going up so many feet without even exerting any energy. How great is this technological innovation? So great. So, so great. Wish I could use it the whole way. But alas, I reach the second level and make my way to the stairs. It takes me *twenty minutes* of climbing. Sure, some people pass me as I stop to catch my breath, but I make it. My legs are on fire. I'm going to be so sore on the plane tomorrow.

I get the shots, including one of the woman who helped Rocky out and her husband clinking their champagne glasses just before they finish off their glasses. Their names are Danielle and Adam and they seem super sweet—both of them are teachers on their summer break. I turn back around and go back down the stairs, this direction going much more quickly—maybe about ten minutes.

On the second floor, I get some assorted shots of the view, the shops, and even the restrooms. I make a pit stop for myself, realizing it's not very often you get to pee this high up. I mean, I guess on an airplane, but it's the freaking *Eiffel Tower*.

Once I'm back down on the ground, I make my way to Rocky's hostel. It is conveniently close to the Musée de l'Orangerie, so I guess I can just grab lunch in that area after I drop off the camera.

The walk there is great to clear my head and organize exactly what I want to say to Rocky. I didn't think I would see him again, so I hadn't planned anything out. I basically blew up at him *again*. After kissing him. Why are my emotions so all over the place today?

I take a deep breath and knock on his door.

Rocky answers it immediately, like he had been sitting there waiting this whole time. "Before you say anything, can I just get some stuff off my chest?"

All of the stuff I had planned to say goes right out the window. I'd rather hear what he has to say. "Sure."

He pulls me into his room with two single beds and sits me down on one of them, sitting himself across from me on the other. "I am really sorry about today. I am so embarrassed that you saw me like that, that you had to change your plans to help me out of a situation I got myself into. I appreciate that you came to help, but I completely understand if it ruined whatever we had between us, seeing me like that."

I stand up, taking his face in my hands to force him to look at me. "I literally did what you did for me at Doge's Palace. I supported you and got you out of there."

"You weren't speechless, getting help from some kid's mom."

I swing my arms out for emphasis. "I literally did that in Munich. And she didn't even speak English."

"Were you curled up like a baby?"

"Fair, but you didn't have anyone to snap you out of it. I can only imagine what I would have been like if you weren't there in Venice or if that mom didn't spot me freaking out."

"Your parents just died. You have reason to freak out. I'm just scared of going too high up."

I kneel down to get closer to Rocky's face. "It's not a competition. You had a panic attack. You needed me and I was there for you, just like you were there for me when I needed you. Needing help doesn't make me love you any less." *Holy shit did I just say what I think I did?* I press my forehead against his. "You brushed your teeth, right?"

He smiles, lifting me up onto his lap to straddle him. "Yeah. Like, three times."

"Good." I press my lips against his, pushing him back onto the bed. It just feels so nice to be in his arms again. I never want to leave. Then again... "I'm on my period."

He threads his fingers through my hair. "I don't mind if you don't."

Okay, that's weirdly hot. "I also have tickets to go see Water Lilies." I look at the clock in the room. "In, like, twenty minutes."

He sits up. "I fucking love Water Lilies. Let's go."

And that is even hotter. "Yeah, let's go."

We get to the museum just in time for our time slot. Rocky thought he was going to have to pull strings to get in, but I still had two tickets, so that made the whole process a bit simpler. The exhibit is even more beautiful than I imagined. We are surrounded by four paintings that look like they were taken straight from a dream. The colors blur together, yet they make a cohesive image from afar. We sit on the bench in the middle of the room, just taking it in. Every once in a while, Rocky gets up to get a closer look at one spot, then comes back down to the bench, his hand finding mine. I am quite content to not look too closely, to admire from where I sit in complete awe. When we finish with one painting, we move to another spot on the bench and do it again. When that room is done, we find the other and start all over.

I could spend hours here in these two rooms. I'm pretty sure we do. Sitting in silence, looking at a piece that must have taken ages. Sitting with Rocky, soaking in the last of our time together.

But then his stomach grumbles. Mine responds. We look at each other and laugh, surprising the visitors around us. We leave, letting everyone else enjoy what we just took in, though likely not in as great of company.

When we hit the fresh air, I turn to Rocky. "Isn't Monet just the best?"

"Monet is great, but I'm more of a Renoir guy myself." Rocky shrugs. "My dad was obsessed with the movie *Amélie* when I was a kid, so *Luncheon of the Boating Party* was kind of my gateway to impressionism."

"I know the painting, but not the movie."

His face falls. "You've never seen *Amélie*?"

I worry that this might be another *Star Wars* moment in that I'm about to be harassed for never having seen it. "No?"

He claps his hands together. "I have it on my computer. We can watch it tonight and then I will take you to Montmartre tomorrow."

He is *really* excited about this. I bite my lip, hesitant to burst his bubble. "I leave tomorrow morning."

His smile falls. After a few seconds, it reappears. "No problem. Dinner in Montmartre tonight, then you can watch the movie whenever you want to remember a great last night in Paris." He pauses. "Hopefully."

I bounce back and forth—settle in for a quiet night and be ready to fly tomorrow, or have one last huzzah with Rocky. It could still feel over if I left right now. I wouldn't long for him. We could ignore what I said in his room. I can just go back to my life, or what's left of it, anyway.

"I really should spend tonight packing. Make sure I have everything ready for tomorrow morning." My heart sinks further into my stomach with each word.

"Oh." Worry crosses his face as he comes to the same realization I do: this is it. "So I guess this is goodbye, then."

I push down the emotion that comes bubbling up. "I guess so."

He grabs my hand. I want him to use it to pull me in and kiss me, but after a moment's hesitation, he brings it to his lips and kisses me gently on the knuckles. "It's been a pleasure spending time with you." He turns away from me, but after only two steps, he turns back around. "I..." He pauses, his brow furrowed, his eyes searching the ground for words. Then he looks me dead in the eyes. "I hope you have a safe trip home."

My breath catches when I realize he did not say what I had been hoping he would. "Thanks."

He gives a resigned smile before turning back around and walking out of my life forever.

I watch him go, disappearing into a crowd.

I make my way to the river—I know if I follow it I will eventually get back to my hotel. I'm not sure how long it will take, but I don't care. If I'm going to be sad and mopey, I'm going to do it with a view—and not while bawling in the back of a rideshare again.

Time passes in a strange manner—when I am lost in thoughts of Rocky, it slows down, as if I'm trying to process every second of my time with him. Why didn't I accept his invitation? Why didn't I directly tell him how I felt? I mean, sure, I used the word *love* at some point, but not in the direct *I love you* sort of way. But I might actually love him. No. I *can't* love him. I just met him. I just found out who he was, like, two days ago. But what I'm feeling is going far beyond what my brain is telling me is possible.

When I near my hotel an hour later, I realize I don't want to go in just yet. My brain wants to punish me just a little longer. Instead, I cross a bridge and walk around a park, meandering through botanical gardens. Half of the stuff in it looks dead from the heat, but the other half is pretty enough. At some points, the plants have outgrown their space, creeping into the walkways, but I just turn back around and find other ways through.

Once I've made a meandering lap, I walk back across the bridge. I want to do one more French thing before I go inside, so

I look up nearby crêpe places. I haven't had one yet and it sounds perfect for a light dinner. It's half a mile to a highly rated crêperie with reviews mostly written in French. It seems promising, so I keep walking.

The crêperie is a little yellow-painted hole in the wall right next to a beautiful courtyard they use as the dining area. My chair wobbles on the cobblestones, and the table does too, but when the ham and cheese crêpe with an egg half-cooked in the center comes out, I manage to keep everything balanced. It is worth the walk—savory, delicious, and just enough to ease the stress of the day. The only problem is the bee who finds my meal just as appetizing as I do. I have to shoo her away on multiple occasions, but then she just goes and harasses other patrons until she is shooed back to me. I eat almost every morsel—all but the one spot the bee had managed to land on. I left it for her to enjoy.

The crêpes are too massive to have yet another for dessert, so I pay and head on my way. It's still a little early, but I do want to be well-rested so I don't accidentally miss the flight. It only takes me an hour to get all of my stuff organized—tomorrow's outfit laid out on the bed, pajamas at the ready, bags packed, and toiletries placed right next to the bag so I can stuff them all inside once I use them.

But it's only 8:00. I sit on the edge of my bed, wondering what to do with myself. I pull out my phone and Google *Amélie.* It's free on one of my streaming services, so I open it.

The rest of the night is spent watching a dreamer helping others and falling in love in Paris. It's so fucking cute. Too fucking cute, in fact. Love doesn't just happen like that. She hardly even knows the guy. He's quirky, she's quirky, and I guess that's endearing, but not something to base an entire relationship on.

Yet by the end of the movie, her happiness is enviable. I find myself shedding tears. I find myself wanting that. I pull up the soundtrack from the movie in my music app and find one of the songs that had stuck in my mind—it's sad but hopeful. It sounds like how moving on from grief feels. It sounds like wanting to be happy. I cry thinking of my dad and my mom. Thinking of Rocky. Thinking of my new life alone.

Chapter 16

Thank goodness I set an alarm because my mixed bag of emotions last night put me into the soundest night of sleep I've gotten in ages. I can barely remember my dream, but I'm pretty sure at one point I was giddily smiling on the back of a bike Rocky was pedaling, zooming through the streets, happy Parisian music playing in the background.

Between each step of getting ready, I hold my phone in my hands, tempted to write a message to Rocky. Each time, I set it back down without doing so. *It's over. The trip, the fling, all of it.*

I lug my bag out to my rideshare and the driver helps me throw it in the trunk. As I sit in the back seat, I look at my phone again. *Just say goodbye.*

Lisa: Hey Rocky. These last two weeks have been—

My phone vibrates in my hand. It's a phone call. From Rocky. My brain short-circuits, forgetting that I need to press a button to answer it, but then it clicks.

"Hello?"

There's massive background noise. "What airline are you on?"

"Uh... Delta. Why?"

"Because I'm at the airport looking for you, but there are so many terminals here and I don't want to miss you." Airplane engines. That's what the sound was.

I sit up in my seat. "I'm not at the airport yet. The app says I'm still about fifteen minutes out."

"I didn't know when your flight was, so I came early. I'll meet you at the Delta counter."

Before I can respond, the call ends. I shake my head. *He already said goodbye. Why would he come to the airport?*

Butterflies bump around in my stomach as I pull up to the terminal. I fumble trying to get my bags onto the sidewalk, my mind in a haze. I see Rocky before I even see the check-in counter. He rushes up to me.

"Don't go."

"What?"

"I love you."

I stand there, staring at him, mouth agape. None of this computes. "I—You what?"

He takes my hands in his. "I couldn't let you go without saying it. I want you to stay. I want us to see if we can make something work between us." He scans my face, loosening his grip on my hands but still holding them in his. "If you don't feel the same way, you can get on your plane and never see me again. I would totally understand."

"Rocky, I—" I take a deep breath, unsure if I can use the same vocabulary he just did, "—feel very strongly for you, too, but if I stay, what then? We just spend a few more days together and have to say goodbye again when that's over? I think it would be easier for us both to just start moving on now."

He lets go completely now. "No. You're right. It's stupid. I just... I'm sorry for coming here and interrupting your day. It was way out of line."

"Rocky..." I start.

"No. No, I'll go. Have a good flight. Maybe text me when you're home so I know you got back safe?"

"Yeah. I can do that." I give him a smile I don't feel.

He just nods once, pauses, then nods again as he turns to go.

I get myself into line, kicking myself the whole time. I just got *another* chance at that whimsical European romance, the happily ever after in Paris. *But it's not real.*

The wait is atrocious. I swear they only have one person working the counter today—maybe someone is out sick. It gives me more time to think, though. More time to realize that I can be happy right now. Maybe it won't last more than a week, but it will be there for now. I don't have to sit alone in my grief. I can go out and have the romantic adventure my mom wanted for me. *She even wrote it into her itinerary.*

When I'm finally up to the counter, the agent asks me to place my bag on the scale.

I can't help but smile. "Actually, I need to rebook my flight for next week."

Epilogue

Well, one week turned into two months. Thank goodness I got a refundable fare, right?

Rocky had another work assignment researching the France, Spain, and Portugal itinerary, then had to take a river cruise to write an article for the Bob Adams website. I got to tag along the whole time and was in charge of taking pictures from the higher vantage points.

Each day was a new adventure and I couldn't imagine going on it with anyone else. In the south of France, I managed to get a massive sunburn at the beach, but Rocky was more than happy to apply aloe *all* over my body. The paella cooking course in Barcelona turned out surprisingly well given that Rocky believes in "measuring with his heart," while I was trying to follow the recipe exactly. We got lost among the plazas and narrow streets of Valencia but we didn't try to catch our bearings too quickly since it was such a nice place to be lost. In Madrid, Rocky convinced me to go to a soccer match—it was an exciting (and loud) experience to say the least, but I am still not sold on the sport just yet. We met up with one of his dad's friends in Lisbon, and he showed us around the colorful city.

The river cruise was much more structured, with only a handful of choices of guided excursions given by the cruise line. I thought I would appreciate it, having timetables and plans, but I've come to find that winging it can be more fun if you're in the right company. Each night we got to retire to our private room for...other attractions...with a view of some of the most beautiful cities I have ever seen.

My work was weirdly accommodating through all of this. Apparently my boss is a hopeless romantic, so once I explained the situation, he let me work remotely. But now my 90 days visa-free in the EU are almost up, and now I am waiting at the airport for my flight home.

Sitting by myself, finishing up the last season of Downton Abbey on my phone, I have little doubt that I love Rocky. So little, in fact, that I will only be back home for about a month until my lease expires. I have some paperwork I need to sign in person to tie up the loose ends of my mom's estate, too. Then I head out to Chicago with my life packed up in my car. I should get there about the same time Rocky gets home so he can help me move into his place. It's not the most logical step, but it *feels* right, and I am going to start making more choices with my heart.

My mom would be so proud.

I still think about her all the time. Slowly, the pain of her memory is being replaced by a warmth—a feeling that a piece of her is always with me—but the waves of grief still come on strong sometimes. I will never stop missing her. It's not like a trip abroad and falling in love would suddenly change that.

I get a text right as I'm about to board.

Rocky: Have a safe flight. I love you.

I roll my eyes, since he's already said goodbye a hundred times, but I respond anyway.

Lisa: Je t'aime. See you stateside.

About the Author

Penny Pentley is a pen name for an author from the Pacific Northwest. Her parents met working at a travel agency and instilled in her a love of European travel. She speaks a little French (poorly) and is prone to panic attacks in confined spaces.

pennypentleybooks@gmail.com

Reviews help independent authors thrive. Please consider rating or reviewing this book.